DUPLEX OCCURRENCE

MARVINA SIMS

ISBN: 978-1-957009-44-5 (sc)
ISBN: 978-1-957009-45-2 (e)

Library of Congress Control Number: 2022903692

Throughout
the 1990's

CHAPTER 1

On a typical day, like yesterday, Sli cranked up the volume on the radio to the sounds of "I Want Her" by Keith Sweat.

I wanther
I want that baby
I wanther
Get it, get it, get it, get it
I wanther
(I wanna do it like this, do it likethat)
I wanther
Once I get it, ain't no turnin' back

You turn me on and on
This feelin,' girl, is so strong
My heart, girl, is on fire
Ooh, you're my desire

I've got a thing for you
Dreams of you and me, baby
She's bad, she's bad, she's bad
All I know is
I want her

Every time she'd gun the engine on the Vibrant Monster, which is the name written on the side of her bike, there goes the same neighbor peeking out the window. Sli glanced up at her, above her shades, and rolled her eyes, instead of waving, emphasizing to her neighbor that she's been seen and ignored on purpose.

After driving a few blocks, Sli stopped to pick up her friend, Felanie, who hopped on the back of the bike. While riding, they both lean forward, further than necessary, to show off their thongs and tattoos, near the cracks of their asses, peeking just above the waist of their jeans.

Sli is what most hood folks would call "thick." Meaning she's not too fat, nor too thin.

Short with a slim upper body, and plump, but tight, hips and ass.

Felanie, on the other hand, is tall, but loosely chunky all over. They both stay dolled up.

Hair done, nails done, er'thang did.

Sli arrived at work and parked her bike. Whenever she has to park further away, she confidently struts by the usual horny gawkers, several homeless beggars and even some female whores, who often proposition her.

If she's in a good mood she may give money to a homeless person and acknowledge hookers with her typical response, "I'm strictly dickly, sweetheart!" However, on days when she's engaged in a heated conversation with Felanie about her deadbeat ass baby daddy, everybody gets ignored.

When she got to the front door of Adisa's Hair Braiding Salon, Big Sheddy was already standing there to let her in.

"Damn! Big Sheddy, what took you so long?" Sli teases.

Big Sheddy smacks his lips while looking down at her from the corner of his eyes, then goes back to sweeping.

But today is not a typical day for Sli because when she goes outside prepared to mount the Vibrant Monster, it's gone. The words *"Whooo. I wonder, wonder, wonder, wonder who?"* from the song "Low Down" by Boz Scaggs runs through Sli's mind. She looks around, up and down the alley. "Aaaah!" Sli screams.

The neighbor peeping from behind the curtain wears a sly grin.

Sli quickly looks up, throwing both of her middle fingers up she yells, "Muthafuck! I feel a war brewing!" Before storming back inside the house.

Sli makes a few phone calls. Minutes later Streng, a friend of the family who lives on the block; Rock, another longtime friend of the family, who lives a half mile away; Felanie and Big Sheddy, who live nearby are her friends and co-workers, and even Sli's twin brother, Snake, are all gathered in Sli's basement apartment.

Snake was the first to arrive since he lives on the second floor of the duplex building. Sli is cooking breakfast. Everyone else is sitting around chatting and watching Sli as she moves about in the kitchen.

"My bike is gone," Sli blurts, waving a spatula in the air.

Snake jerks his head. "That's why you called us, or rather me, to come down here?" He asks, wrinkling his eyebrows. "Whatchu think? One of us stole it?"

"Ha! If I even thought one of yall had it I'd be fuckin' ya up right now and askin' questions later. Naw but I thought about Grenely was doing work for mama a few days ago and figured it must've been him since the word is he's strung out now." Sli sets a plate of grits, eggs, sausage and biscuits on the table before yelling, "Bryk…Food ready!"

Rock, who is in conversation with Streng, stops talking mid-sentence, jumps up quickly from his seat. "I'm gon' fix my plate."

"Wait! What? No, you not." Sli says.

Rock stops in his tracks. "How the fuck you gon' cook a whole southern breakfast, call us to come over to help you, and not even offer us shit? You called us all over here for something *you* want help with and aint even gon' feed us?"

Streng, who had not heard what Rock said, butts in. "I'm glad you cooked bweakfast. I didn't eat. Rushed ova here, figuwing it was a emergency." Streng is hearing impaired and has difficulty pronouncing certain letters, or saying entire words clearly, but he reads lips well. He is so extremely thin that even when he's wearing a belt, he has to constantly keep pulling his pants up.

"I don't know how none of yall niggas thought that shit! Yall asses shoulda ate fo' ya got here." Sli says in between chewing. "Bryk! Come eat! Anyway, like I said, I believe Grenely got my bike."

Bryk walks out of his bedroom in his pajamas. He is Sli's only eight-year-old son. He's bigger and taller than the average kid his age.

Snake lightly kicks Bryk on the butt as he passes by. "Li' rude ass boy. You speak when you enter a room."

"Hey, Uncle Snake." Bryk says, as if his jaws are wired. He grabs his plate and pulls a chair from the kitchen table, about to sit down across from Sli.

"Uh un." Sli says, quickly stopping him. "Gone on back to yo room. You got my permission this time but don't make it no habit though."

As Bryk is walking back to his room Snake snatches Bryk's plate. Bryk looks at him nonchalantly. Snake takes a bacon and returns the plate. Bryk stares at his plate, turns to look back toward the kitchen, wondering if he should get another piece of bacon, but then just heads toward his bedroom, and closes the door.

Sli continues eating. Everyone is staring at her.

"Damn you really aint gon' offer us no food for real." Big Sheddy says. Big Sheddy is tall and obese with unkempt dreadlocks. He's a bit of a scatter brain but helps the entire family out, which is why his loyalty sways, based on who needs him in the moment.

Sli, continues chewing, looks at each of them before responding. "Fuck naw 'cause I know yall gon' say yeah. So, what we gon' do 'bout my bike?"

Did you call the police?" Big Sheddy asks. Everybody looks at him like he personally offended them.

Streng loudly releases his tongue from the roof of his gums. "Maaan, what da fuuu they gone do? They don't even give a shit 'bout us, da fu' you think they gon' care 'bout a nigga bike?"

Big Sheddy humps his shoulders in response. "So, what you wanna do?" Snake asks.

Sli scrapes the excess food particles from her plate into the garbage can. "Go get him so we can find out what he did with my bike."

"But you're dubious as to if he even got your bike." Felanie says.

"Well, there's only one way to find out, aint it, Ms. Dictionary?" Sli says. Rock, Big Sheddy and Streng stand, and begin walking toward the door. "Since you finish can we get yo leftovers fuwst?" Streng asks.

"Boy…Get yo ass on outta here." Sli raises her foot attempting to kick Streng in the ass.

Streng yells, "What da fuuu." while twisting his hips to successfully dodge Sli's foot. His pants fall around his ankles. He bends over quickly to pull them back up, then thrusts his hips forward, figuring she would attempt to kick him again.

They leave out the basement in search of Grenely.

CHAPTER 2

Grenely is standing in front of a liquor store with other guys. They take turns taking a swig from a bottle wrapped in a brown paper bag. With Grenely being the neighborhood hustling handyman, no request is off limits for the type of work he's willing to do. So, he's more than anxious to do something strange for a little bit of change.

Rock approaches Grenely. "Yo…Grene. Sli say she gotta job she wantchu to handle…Like right now."

Grenely jerks his head upward in acknowledgement, puts up a finger, and takes a swig from the bottle. "A'ight let her know I'll be there in a few."

Rock tightens his lips and shakes his head with held back frustration. Big Sheddy and Streng walk up behind Rock. "Naw dude. That's not gon' work," Big Sheddy says.

Rock looks around. "Unless he changed the definition of *now*," Rock chuckles.

Grenely squints his eyes in bafflement. Shifting his gaze between the three of them, he gives the bottle to the man standing next to him and walks away with Rock, Streng and Big Sheddy.

They head back toward Sli's apartment, which is in the basement of the duplex apartment building where Haddie Maldive and her youngest daughter, Diana Maldive, are sitting on the porch. Haddie owns the building. She and Diana live in the first-floor apartment. Snake and Sli are Haddie's twin son and daughter.

A bell is heard faintly jingling up the street. It gets louder as it nears the building. "Oh, good here comes the bike man." Diana says excitedly as she descends the steps.

"Now I don't have to walk to no sto'. I've been wanting me some sunflower seeds all day." As the man on the bike is approaching, he's loudly announcing:

Fresh off the freight, so you know it's great!
My name is Cooper, but you can call me Coop.
Accessories: from bangles, bags to boots.
Got toys for yo' kids that can spin, sang, or shoot.
Wanna eat?
Got those sour, sugary, and salty treats.
Need something at home?
Check out my cutlery, candles, brushes and combs.
If you need it, and I don't got it, just let it be known.
I'll cop it when I can. I SWEAR the wait won't be long.
Be back here in a flash; sangin' this same ole song.

Just as Coop is approaching the duplex, Diana waves to get his attention then runs into the street to stop him. She buys the sunflower seeds and returns to sit on the porch to eat them.

Coop stares at Haddie. "How you doing, Ms. Lady?"

"Fairly middling. And you?" Haddie says as she fans herself with an envelope. "Making a living. Is there anything you need today?" Coop asks, wiping sweat fromhis forehead with a handkerchief.

"Only about a million dollars." Haddie replies. "I'll put the order in to rob a bank for ya."

Haddie and Diana laugh. Coop winks as he peddles away. Haddie and Diana wave.

Rock, Streng, Big Sheddy and Grenely walk up the steps. Haddie continues fanning herself. She gets a big smile upon seeing Grenely.

"Where yall done found Grenely at? Grenely I been lookin' for you all last week. The toilet on my handle broke and Diana's bedroom door is starting to come off the hinges..."

Diana chuckles. "The toilet on your handle broke, Ma?"

Streng and Big Sheddy continue walking into the basement. Grenely stops to listen. Rock stands beside him.

"Aw shut up!" Haddie quickly swats her makeshift fan toward Diana. "Yall know what the hell I mean," Haddie says chuckling.

"No worries, Mama Haddie. I'll take care of er'thang you want after the fourth of July, when I get back from visiting my family down home. Mama been tryna get me to come back to Arkansas for years and I finally got a ride now."

"What part of Arkansas you from?" Haddie asks. "Greasy Corner."

Haddie Jerks her head in shock. "So that's a real place? Nodding, Grenely answers. "Yes ma'am."

Haddie lets out a piercingly loud laugh. "You know my kid's daddy said he was from Greasy Corner. I thought that nigga was just fuckin' wit' me. Tryna say he was slick or some shit. But it looks like he was dead serious. A city with a name like that must specialize in all types of grease—butter, lard, fat back, ham hocks, bacon, chitlins, matter of fact a pig's er'…" She bursts out laughing again. Rock and Grenely smile.

"Ma you need to stop." Diana says in between chuckles.

"Well now, that explains why both of yall asses the color of charcoal after it's been burning a while, 'cause ya both look like ya fell in a grease trap then stood staring at the sun in an open cornfield frying ya own black asses." Haddie stands up mockingly staring at the sky, with her neck extended as if asking the sun to burn her. She releases another piercingly loud laughter, then going silent from not being able to catch her breath.

She continues trying to talk, while forcing back more laughter. "But you know what…that still don't explain…why yall feet and hands be so crusty? Lookin' like yall been slapping and kick boxing concrete and bricks" Haddie swings her arms and kicks her legs "Lost each round and kept going back for another new and improved ass whooping."

Haddie and Diana are loudly laughing. Rock and Grenely chuckle.

Rock lightly shoves Grenely and beckons his head toward Sli's basement door to get him to go inside the building.

Grenely excuses himself. "A'ight Mama Haddie I'll be coming back over to help you out."

Haddie is still laughing too hard to respond. She waves in a way that looks more like she's trying to fan herself, but at the same time acknowledging Grenely.

****

When Grenely steps through the basement door Big Sheddy grabs him in a headlock. Grenely struggles to get loose and is trying to talk but his words are muffled. The song "The Ghetto" by Too Short is playing.

Even though the streets are bumpy, lights burned out
Dope fiends die with a pipe in their mouths
Old school buddies not doing it right
Every day it's the same
And it's the same every night
I wouldn't shoot you, bro, but I'd shoot that fool
If he played me close and tried to test my cool
Every day I wonder just how I'll die
Only thing I know is how to survive
There's only one rule in the real world
And that's to take care of you, only you and yours
Keep dealing with the hard times day after day
Might deal me some dope, but then crime don't play
Black man tried to break in my house again
Thought he got off the dope doing time in the pen
Even thought my brothers do me just like that
I get a lot of love so I'm giving it back to the ghetto.
The ghetto (talking 'bout the ghetto)
The ghetto (funky, funky ghetto)
The ghetto (tryin' to live our lives)
The ghetto…

Big Sheddy slams Grenely down into a folding chair. Rock and Snake hold Grenely's legs down as they strap them to the legs of the chair with duct tape. Streng holds Grenely's hands behind his back while Felanie tapes them together. Grenely is protesting and trying to getfree.

Felanie smacks duct tape across his mouth.

Snake, Big Sheddy, Streng and Rock take turns beating Grenely. Sli and Felanie are watching. Grenely's face is bloody. Sli snatches the tape from Grenely's mouth. Bryk peeks out of his bedroom door.

"Where's my bike, Grenely?"

"Come on Sli…now you know damn well I wouldn't take nothin' from you. Yall pay me enough to work around here I don't need to steal nothin' from yall." Grenely pants.

"Yeah well, you gettin' quite the reputation around here. I hear you're strung out now.

Crack heads'll do anythang to get they shit." Sli jumps, then bends over with her hands gripping her knees. She widens her eyes as she looks into Grenely's face.

Sli walks away and grabs a bat from a corner, twirling it like a baton. "So, where's my shit! Stripped and scattered at the junk yard? Or just stripped? Or did you trade it whole for a hit?"

"But Sli, I wouldn't do…"

"Shut the fuck up!" Sli strikes Grenely on his head with the bat. He goes silent as his head slumps backward.

Bryk closes the bedroom door silently.

Snake, Big Sheddy, Streng and Rock take Grenely's body from the chair, wrap it in plastic and drag it behind the couch.

"Yall be sure to come right back here tonight to help me get rid of him." Sli tells them.

****

As soon as the sun goes down, they are all in the backyard, shoveling, digging a circular shaped grave.

After about an hour of not digging deep enough, Rock throws his shovel down. "Maaan, fuck this. It'll be daylight before we can dig deep enough. I'm gonna call my boy. He works for the city. He'll hook us up with something."

They all go back inside. Minutes later Rock is chatting on the phone. He hangs up. "Okay. He say I gotta meet him. And that's perfect 'cause we don't need no mo' witnesses."

"Meet him for what? What's going on?" Sli asks.

"You'll see when I get back. I need to meet him at his job where he got access to the equipment we need. He's getting off soon, and I don't want to miss him. Only one of yall can go with me though."

"Da fuck, Rock! I don't like all this secrecy shit!" Sli yells as Rock is walking toward the door.

"Ya just gonna have to trust me baby girl." Rock turns back to walk up close to Sli, gazing down at her as she stares back into his eyes.

Snake looks perturbed. He jumps up from his seat. "I'll ride withchu." Sli walks away. When they get outside, Snake asks, "What the fuck was all that about?"

"All what?" Rock feigns stupid. "Yeah okay," Snake says.

****

An hour later there's a loud beeping sound in the backyard. Sli jumps up from the couch to look out the window. "Da fuck…a construction truck is backing up into the backyard! I swear this better be them." Sli goes outside. Everyone else follows. Rock is driving a drilling rig. Snake is standing next to the vehicle.

Streng is giggling and jumping with excitement, pacing back and forth. "Daaamn man!

You need to let me take a spin in dis mufucka!" Streng walks up to Rock. "Come on maaaan! Let me get a turn!"

"Nigga this aint no Destruction Derby video game! Get yo ass back!" Rock yells as he continues drilling.

Rock stops drilling. Snake, Big Sheddy and Streng bring Grenely's body outside and drop him into the hole so that it is standing straight up. Rock is cursing himself when he notices Grenely's hair is sticking up a half inch above the hole.

"Man don't trip. We got enough dirt to keep that fool covered." Snake assures him. They shovel dirt back into the hole.

That same neighbor is peeping out the window.

CHAPTER 3

Bob Marley's "Three Little Birds (Don't Worry About a Thing)" is playing as Sli and other stylists are braiding hair. Sli finishes braiding a customer's hair then spins the chair around so that she can look at herself in the mirror atop the vanity table. The customer, Nicky, smiles as she turns her head at different angles to admire her new look.

"Girrrlfriend! This shit is hot! You worked a miracle making the hairstyle cuter than me.

Biiiiitch this shit is off the hoooook!" Nicky laughs, moving her lips and teeth excessively. "Yaaasss bitch! I told you I was gonna hook you up…again!" Sli says.

Just as Nicky goes into her purse for money to pay Sli, the bells over the door jingle. A girl walks in. Sli looks at the door and smiles. "Whatchu doin' here Tawny?"

Walking up to Sli Tawny speaks in an innocent voice. "My daddy say let him hold fifty dollars 'til he get off work tonight,"

"Tell yo' daddy he still owe me a hunerd dollars from the last time he didn't pay me all my money back."

Tawny runs back outside.

"She's a cutie. How old is she?" Nicky asks. "Eleven going on thirty-eleven," Sli says.

Adisa, the owner of the hair salon, is braiding a customer's hair when she looks up and stares at Sli some seconds before addressing her in her thick and abrasive African accent. "Dat door should be lawked! Peeple see her runnin' in and out dey dink dey can walk-in too. You need to go out dere; handle yo' own bezness." Adisa's tone lowers when she begins speaking in her Native language to the stylist who is helping her braid.

"Relax, Adisa. My niece ain't gon' stick this joint up," Sli says. "I'll lock it as soon as she leaves for good." Sli looks over at Big Sheddy, and rolls her eyes, as she continues justifying her case. "Even though that's Big Sheddy's job to keep that door locked. Not mine."

Big Sheddy looks up from sweeping with frustration to stare at Sli. He then looks around in embarrassment at everyone. "Now how you gon' just put me out there like that?"

"Don't worry 'bout it, Big Sheddy," Sli says as she rolls her eyes at Adisa, then speaks under her breath to Nicky. "This bitch is workin' my nerves. Almost got enough money to get my own shop. My realtor is helping me look into some places. Oh…I better give you this 'cause it could be any day now." Sli reaches into a drawer. Nicky gives Sli money as Sli hands her a business card. Sli continues speaking softly. "This is my cell phone number. If you call here and they tell you I don't work here no mo' call me directly to make yo' appointment."

Tawny returns. This time skipping up to Sli. "He say okay he gon' give it all to you tonight when he get home."

Sli tilts her head, staring puzzled, as she moves closer toward Tawny's face. Sli slaps Tawny then grabs one of her ears. Tawny screams. Everyone in the salon has a different reaction—shocked, disgust or unmoved.

"These my muthafuckin' earrings!" Sli yells. She continues holding Tawny's ear while pulling her out the door. Tawny is crying as they head toward Snake's car. The commotion causes people to stare.

"I don't know where yo' li' ass get off thinking you can mess with my shit!" They stop at Snake's car. Snake is on the phone. He stops talking when he hears the fuss. Sli bends down to talk to Snake through his passenger side window while still holding Tawny's ear. "Get control of yo' thieving ass child! This li' heifer is wearing my diamond earrings."

Snake speaks into the phone. "Dawg, let me call you back." He jumps out of the car. "Okay, Sli! Damn! Let her go!" Snake jerks Tawny's arm. Sli releases her. Tawny hugs Snake as she cries with her face in his chest.

"It aint that serious. You buggin' over a pair of earrings!"

"Ya damn straight I'm buggin! Those goddamn diamonds aint cheap!" Snake starts taking the earrings out of Tawny's ears.

"Oh hell naw! I don't want that shit back. Yo' baby mama probably been wearin' them too! And whatever other hoochies they associate with!"

Snake bawls up his fists. "Maaan…you…Come on Tawny get in the car." He assists Tawny into the passenger seat, then walks to get back into the driver's seat.

Sli quickly throws loose bills into the car totaling fifty dollars. "Now you owe me sixteen hunerd!"

Snake yells, "Fuck you!" as he pulls off burning rubber. "Naw you the one fucked if I don't get all my stash back!"

CHAPTER 4

Haddie and Diana alternate between tending to the meat on the grill, going in and out of the building, preparing dishes inside, then bringing out various platters of food. Streng is walking up the gangway, heading into Haddie's backyard.

Tia is walking a few feet behind Streng. Tia is the flamboyant and sassy neighbor, with a full beard and mustache, who wears various styles and colored wigs. When she steps into the yard she yells, "Happy Independence Day everybody! Even though all our Black asses still slaves." She laughs loudly.

Streng approaches Haddie as she is carrying out a dish. "How you doin' Ms. Haddie?

You want me to help you wit' sumin, Ms. Haddie?"

"Yeah. Take this and put it over there on the table. Where dat Grenely at? He would've been here by now helping us out." Streng fakes a chuckle then raises his eyebrows.

Diana, who is carrying a dish to the table, responds to Haddie. "Ma you must've forgot he said he was gonna see his Mama in Arkansas."

"Oh, that's right. That greasy nigga *did* say he was going to Greasy Corner." Haddie bursts out laughing.

Diana chuckles. "Ma, please don't start that up again. We got too much to finish."

Tia interposes, using her wrists to flip her hands in different directions, intended only to prove exaggerated femininity. Though Tia is stocky from head to waist she's pretty wide and jiggly from the waist down. "Hey, Ms. Haddie, I can help you out too. What else you need to be done?"

"Hey Tia. Come inside. I'll show you." Haddie yells out.

Throughout the yard kids are dancing, running around, throwing water balloons. Both kids and adults are hula hooping and jumping double Dutch. Adults are eating, dancing, conversing, laughing, drinking, smoking or just staring at what everybody else is doing.

A game of spades is being played at the card table. Sli and Rock, sit across from each other as partners. Just as Jessica and Snake are partners and sitting across from each other.

Jessica is Snake's twins' mama.

Diana, Haddie and Tia continue going back and forth, carrying trays of food outside. Haddie places a dish on the table and is heading back inside. Tia, holding items in her hands, stops on top of the circular dirt where Grenely is buried. She scrapes the bottom of her shoe around it and goes in circles on top of it. She averts her eyes back and forth from the group at the spades table to Haddie. "Ms. Haddie! What happened to yo grass right here?"

Haddie stops to look at the spot with Tia. Sli, Streng, Snake and Rock look at Tia then at each other. Tia slowly looks at each of them with a smirk.

"You need to look into this 'cause you didn't always have this patch of grass missing.

Did you?" Tia continues.

"Naw. I don't know what happened there." Haddie says with a puzzled look as she too begins swiping her shoe across the dirt patch.

"And I'm sure this didn't just happen today, even with all these people walking around here." Tia says as she continues looking, with a smirk, at those sitting at the card table.

"You right about that. I don't know how that could've happened," Haddie agrees.

Enjoying the tension, Tia continues. "And I know we aint got no gophers 'round here in the hood. Now I would say it could be a possum or a raccoon done dug itself a hole but we in the hood where mostly the country folks live so I know all the possums and coons done got shot and eaten for Thanksgiving. Hell, the only rodents brave enough to still hang around here is the rats. And I know they could get huge but aint none around here hardly that big and round either. But you know what…there are rabbits round here too, but even they aint near bout that big." Tia lets out a loud and long laugh, which causes her to bend over. When she finally stands straight and calms down, she looks at Haddie with seriousness and asks, "What you think Ms. Haddie?" Tia again glares over at Sli, Streng, Snake and Rock with a smirk.

"I don't know, chile. I'll look into it later. I'm glad you pointed that out. Now gone put that stuff on the table so we can hurry up and finish." Haddie says shooing Tia.

Sli, Snake, Streng and Rock display various versions of their growling faces as they stare with irritation and discomfort at Tia.

The song "Treat 'Em Right" by Chubb Rock plays.

> *Go, go, go, go, go, go, go*
> *Go, go, go, go, go, go, go*
> *Nineteen ninety, Chubb Rock jumps up on the scene*
> *With a lean and a pocket full of green*
> *The green doesn't symbolize I made it on the top*
> *But Robocop last year was a shock*

Nearby, Big Sheddy stands the top of a bat on the ground, bends over to place his forehead on the bottom of the handle of the bat, then spins himself around in circles. He stops spinning and tries to stand straight. Fighting with gravity to remain standing, he stumbles like a drunk, falling face down onto the card table.

Streng runs over to the card table, pointing at Big Sheddy. "What the fuuu!" Streng laughs loudly, then falls on his knees, continuing to taunt Big Sheddy.

Tia is drinking but spits it out laughing loudly. "What the hell? His big ass can't handle his liquor he needs to join Alcoholics Anonymous like yester year."

A man standing next to turns to Tia to say, "Big Sheddy don't even drink alcohol." Tia looks at him with disgust. "Like I give a fuck."

Snake and Jessica jump up from the card table irritated. "Maaan… the fuck is yo big ass playing childish games fo'!" Snake yells. "Yo ass is entirely too big fa dis shit. Getcho yo big ass up…Shit!" Snake tries, extensively, to push Big Sheddy from the table but fail. Big Sheddy's body jiggles. Jessica tries lifting him as if she is stronger than Snake.

Rock and Sli are laughing uncontrollably. "Shiiit you gon' need a fucking crane to pull that big nigga up." Rock says holding his stomach.

Big Sheddy finally lifts himself and stands up to watch the card game, as does Streng. The cards are scattered everywhere along with the money. There is a pot for the winning team and another one for the individual with the highest spade. The players begin arguing as tohow many books they each had and who won the lastbook.

"Since we can't get this settled it's a do over." Sli says as she throws her cards face up onto the table.

Rock jumps up. "Aw come one now Sli…Shit! Why the fuck you do that? I was about to run a boston on these fools." He sits back down as he shows his hand. "I get that high spades pot tho' 'cause I had all four of them aces."

"Wait a minute…hold on." Snake holds one hand out to keep Rock from grabbing the money as he looks through the book of cards. "A'ight." Snake says, as if satisfied with his own conclusion.

A drunk man is staggering by the table when he blurts out, "Yall need to take that shit outside." Everybody looks at him with confusion. Some chuckle.

"Who the fuck is you?" Sli asks.

The drunk man sways in place struggling to respond. "I…I… toldchu…You forgot that fast," the drunk man says, throwing his arms in the air. "Listen here…" After swiftly batting his eyes, he closes them while raising his eyebrows. He takes a deep breath then loudly releases it for a long time. Everyone scrunches their faces, while some either pinch their nostrils or turn their heads away. The drunk man finally continues his slurred speech. "The only reason ice cubes can make warm water so cold is 'cause yo' warm hands be on the outside of the cup." He offers Sli his cup. Sli stares at him. The drunk man then tries to walk away but staggers in circles.

"Hey Ma!" Snake yells interrupting Haddie's conversation. She turns to look at him. "Who this is?" Snake points to the drunk man. Haddie shakes her head and humps her shoulders.

Tia rushes to stand next to Haddie and yells out, "Aint he related to Grenely?" A grin spreads across Tia's face.

Jessica raises her eyebrows, and ask, "Grenely got folks living here?" No one responds. Jessica humps her shoulders. As the others at the table are looking at each other uncomfortably, Tia busts up loudly laughing for too long. Sli begins mean mugging Tia.

Sli rolls her eyes at Tia then addresses everyone at the card table. "This dude had to be bent when he walked back here 'cause er'body else aint even really got started drinking yet,"

"Yo Big Sheddy! Gone handle my light weight!" Rock yells.

Big Sheddy snatches the drunk man's collar causing him to stumble and fall. Everyone is laughing and chuckling, but Streng is the loudest and laughs the longest.

"Wait! Hold on now! You done made me spill my drank!" The drunk man protests. "Who deal is it?" Jessica asks.

"Sli." Rock and Snake say in unison.

When Sli finishes shuffling and dealing out the cards, everyone takes time rearranging the cards in their hands. Jessica is about to throw one down but hesitates, looks around the yard, then at Snake with a puzzled look before asking, "Speaking of Grenely…Where he at?"

Snake, Sli, Rock, Big Sheddy and Streng sneakily look at one another. Snake humps his shoulders. Big Sheddy raises his eyebrows looking down at all of them.

"Oh yeah, um, Diana just said Grenely went to Arkansas to see his Mama." Streng says attempting to break the tension.

Rock nods his head, "Oooh…yeeeah…that's right. What he said." pointing at Streng. "Yall sho bout that?" Tia asks. Everyone looks over at her, as she seems to have magically appeared. She then walks away loudly laughing and clapping her hands.

Jessica, content with the answer to Grenely's absence says, "Oh, I knew it had to be something..." Snake rolls his eyes in his head, but Jessica continues. "...'Cause yall know it wouldn't be like Grenely to miss out on nothing free..." Snake looks at Jessica with irritation. Jessica cluelessly keeps talking. "...Especially when lots of food and liquor..."

"Just gone play yo damn hand. It's yo turn." Snake snaps. Jessica gives him that oh-no-you-didn't Sista girl look.

"Hey! Who dog is this?" Haddie yells out. There is a dog digging on the dirt patch where Grenely is buried.

People turn to look at what Haddie is referring to. Snake's mouth flies open, Rock slaps his forehead then wipes the side of his face, Sli throws her cards face down onto the table, Big Sheddy whispers under his breath, "Oh shit!" at the same time Streng yells out, "What the fuuuu!"

"Pootanaaaanny! Pooooootanaaaanny! Pootananny! Get over here!" Tia yells from a distance before walking over to look down at the dog. "What are you doing, Pootananny? You know you aint supposed to be digging in other people's yard. Ms. Haddie dogs usually can sniff out thangs. You think he's trying to get a bone from under there or something?" Tia swiftly turns her head to the card table, grinning mischievously.

"Aint no bones got no business being buried in my yard," Haddie tells her.

Streng runs over to snatch the dog up. He shoves it into Tia's chest. Tia bursts into laughter.

****

Before night falls someone has placed several orange cones at each end of the block to stop traffic.

A neighbor is heard fussing. "Whoever put them damned cones down already I told yall to wait 'cause Terrinika is on her way home from work. Now she gon' have to park far away and walk, pregnant with twins. I should call the police on yall assess!"

Someone yells out, "Shiiit, Ms. Turner seeing that this Terrinika's seventeenth pregnancy. She'll be able to just pop thoses li mufukas out in her own hands, even if she is walking down the block so those cones may be doing her a favor!"

People nearby are laughing.

"Tia I know that aint nobody but yo ignant ass. You just mad 'cause you can't get pregnant. Aintchu boy?

Some people respond with "Ooooo."

The block is jammed packed as people are either standing and sitting on their own porches, their neighbor's porches, in the streets and on the sidewalks, or either leaning or sitting on parked vehicles.

Fireworks are blasting from the nearby vacant lot as people are gaping toward the sky yelling, "oooh," "aaaw," and even cheering. The loudest booms keep setting off car alarms, creating a vibration on the ground, and even rattling the windows in some people's homes.

CHAPTER 5

Ruby walks deliberately slowly, while judgmentally staring at different things and people over the top of her glasses. She stops at the bottom of the steps in front of Haddie's wrought iron gate, where Haddie is fanning herself with a tattered notebook. Ruby looks around to be sure no one is in earshot. "Hey now, Haddie?"

"What's the latest Ms. Ruby?"

Ruby looks around again before whispering loudly. "You know Gerald got a lawsuit against the city. He drove into that big pothole at the corner. Busted his transmission wide open. He say he suffered a concussion and had some hemorrhaging on the brain 'cause he hit his head on his windshield winda." Someone walks by. Ruby stops talking and watches them until they pass. "Now don't start me to lying but I believe he just tryna get a disability check. And since he hit his head, if he really did, they gon' question him why he didn't have his seatbelt on and proly aint gon' give him shit. I tell ya…as long as that gon' take for Social Security to decide if he's el'gible or not, if he don't die first, he gon' mess around and lose his house. Watch what I tell ya." She looks down at her feet shaking her head. Then looks up at Haddie while throwing her hand toward heaven. "Sho as God is my witness…. And you know what else I believe? Gerald just tryna get some free meals from me, but he betta carr' his ass on down to that welfare line like the rest of his kin folk. I sho hate the Marillac House stopped giving away powered milk and free blocks of cheese though."

"Who cut the cheese?"

Ruby, jumps and jerks her head around swiftly to see Tia standing uncomfortably close to her. "Boy! Where you come from?"

Tia rolls her eyes. Her pupils remain frozen toward her forehead as her head bobbles. "You so disrespectful. Hey Ms. Haddie."

Haddie smiles. "Whatcha know good, Tia?"

Before opening her mouth Tia begins jiggling her head, swinging her arms, and flicking her wrists. "I'm so sick of Ms. Turner smart ass mouth. Alls I know is if one mo' of those Turner bitches at 2742 gets pregnant again I'm personally bum rushing in there to give all they asses my personalized tubal ligation process." Tia begins gesturing her intended actions by exaggeratedly using her hands to make it look as if she's spreading someone's legs and stab their vagina with an object. "Then I'll reach inside all they coochies, snatch all they ovaries out, burn 'em, stomp on 'em and then politely put 'em right back inside." She stops abruptly, panting as if out of breath. "But what I really wanna know is where is all them folks sleeping at anyway? 'Cause ALL they boyfriends living there too. I bet most of they asses gotta be sleepin' on theflo'."

Haddie butts in. "Or *on top* of each other." She giggles.

Tia and Ruby turn up their lips, raising their eyebrows as if trying to picture the arrangement, then nod in agreement.

"And therein *lies* the problem." Tia says, then bursts out laughing. "Y'all get it…lies…like lie down." No one responds. "Aw just forget it," Tia says.

"Naw now…Don't start me to lying but I saw them taking some of those cots in there.

You know like how they have down at the homeless shelter?" Ruby says half asking, half stating.

Haddie gets a confused look on her face. "So, whatchu saying Ruby is they living like they homeless inside they own home." Haddie chuckles.

"That's exactly what it sounds like to me." Tia agrees and bursts out laughing loudly and long. Everyone joins in.

Ms. Ruby continues. "Yall don't believe me, then ask Grenely. He…"

"Speaking of Grenely. Has anybody seen him lately? Tia interrupts. She then stares at Haddie.

"Well…now that you mention it…I sho aint seen him. I thought he would've been back from visiting his Mama down south by now."

"Shonuff? Where south?" Ruby asks. "Greasy Corner."

"Quit playin', Ms. Haddie." Ruby says.

"I shit ya not. That's what he told me. I thought it was a joke too 'cause I first heard of it from my kids father. Oooh, I was cuttin' they asses up when Grenely said they slick asses actually lived in a place with a name like that. I couldn't…"

"Oh yeah, he went down south all right. So, did he say when he was coming back?" Tia interrupts to steer the topic back.

"He didn't say." Haddie scratches her breast, near her underarm. "He just told me he gon' see his mom for the holiday and he'd help me around the house when he got back."

"Tia what you mean 'he went down south all right?'" You said that like you know something," Ruby says.

Tia ignores her. "Sooo, Ms. Haddie, you don't think something happened to him, especially since he aint been back to your house to make some loot? 'Cause you know how crack heads need that cash."

Bells are jingling as Cooper rides his bike nearby. They turn their heads in his direction. "Speaking of crackheads…" Tia continues. "Damn, that's one homeless man that be everywhere. Most homeless people stay put in a spot where they can make it feel like home."

"Now how you figurin' that man a homeless crackhead?" Ruby interjects. "'Cause the crackheads I know don't know how to handle business the way Coop does."

"Huh? You must aint seent him?" Tia retorts.

"Kinda question is that? There aint nobody around here who aint seent him." Ruby mocks.

Haddie jumps in. "That don't mean nothin' now, Tia 'cause on the news they caught people looking raggedy and begging. And when they was done hustling they use they push button car remote on they luxurious vehicles, then drive on home to they luxurious mansions. And probably got yachts parked on Lake Shore Drive and private jets, flying them across country and who knows whatever other shit we workin' po' folks can't afford but still aint begging to get it."

Tia squints her eyes as she tries to see which way Coop is going. "Oh well maybe he's heading to his mansion now, in that cardboard box, since he aint even comin' this way. Looks like he kept on down California."

They each give the look and gesture of oh well, either tilting their head, raising their eyebrows, and humping their shoulders.

CHAPTER 6

A LATE AFTERNOON AT GARFIELD PARK'S BASKETBALL COURT

I can feel it coming in the air tonight, (Oh lord)
And I've been waiting for this moment, for all my life, (Oh lord)
Can you feel it coming in the air tonight, oh lord, (Oh lord)
Well, if you told me you were drowning
I would not lend a hand
I've seen your face before my friend
But I don't know if you know who I am
Well, I was there and I saw what you did
I saw it with my own two eyes
So you can wipe off that grin, I know where you've been
It's all been a pack of lies…

The song, "In the Air Tonight" by Phil Collins is blaring from a vehicle's speakers.

Snake, Sli, Bryk, Tyler, Tawny, Felanie, Streng and Rock are teamed up, playing basketball and talking shit. Big Sheddy along with others are on the sidelines watching. Two people are fidgeting with their basketballs, waiting for the game to end.

Gun shots ring out. Some people run, while others dive to the ground. Sli lies over her nephew, Tyler, to shield him, as Snake lies over his nephew, Bryk, protecting him. Snake looks around for his daughter Tawny and sees Rock is safeguarding her.

Once the shooting finally ends. People cautiously lift their heads to look around.

A blood curdling scream is heard.

AN EARLY DAWN AT GARFIELD PARK CONSERVATORY

> *Summer, summer, summertime*
> *Time to sit back and unwind*
> *Summertime*
> *Here it is the groove slightly transformed*
> *Just a bit of a break from the norm*
> *Just a little somethin' to break the monotony…*

The song "Summertime" by DJ Jazzy Jeff & the Fresh Prince is blasting from a SUV's speakers. Snake, Sli, Diana, Bryk, Tyler, Tawny, Felanie, Rock, Streng and Big Sheddy are fishing. Tyler pulls his line up to show the tiny fish he'd caught and begins excitedly jumping around.

"Dude…Yo exhilaration level is superfluously over the top," Felanie says.

Everyone laughs. Sli smacks Tyler on the back of his head. Tyler winces and grabs his head. "Ooouch!"

Snake looks irritated with Sli. Snake and Diana exchange looks.

Seeing Snake's disapproval gives Diana the courage to speak up. "Damn Sli you didn't have to smack him that hard."

Sli looks at Diana and rolls her eyes. Then directs her attention to Tyler. "That fish aint even fully developed enough inside for anybody to even bother with gutting it, so it damn sho aint enough of it to get YO greedy ass full."

Sli looks at Diana then jumps at her as if she's going to hit her. Diana gives Sli that I- wish-you-would Sista girl look.

Snake snatches the fish from Tyler's line and throws it back in the water. They continue fishing.

AN EVENING AT THE CHICAGO STADIUM

…Thinkin' back on my one-room shack
Now my mom pimps a Ac' with minks on her back
And she loves to show me off, of course
Smiles every time my face is up in The Source

We used to fuss when the landlord dissed us
No heat, wonder why Christmas missed us
Birthdays was the worst days
Now we sip champagne when we thirsty

Damn right I like the life I live
'Cause I went from negative to positive
And it's all, it's all good
And if you don't know, now you know, you know
You know very well who you are

Don't let 'em hold you down, reach for the stars
(And if you don't know, now you know, you know)
You had a goal, but not that many
'Cause you're the only one, I'll give you good and plenty
(And if you don't know, now you know)

The song, "Juicy" by Notorious B.I.G is blaring through the Chicago Stadium's speakers as Snake, Sli, Diana, Bryk, Tyler, Tawny, Felanie, Big Sheddy, Rock and Streng are taking their seats. The crowd stands, screaming with excitement, as the Chicago Bulls scramble about, taking the lead in the final's basketball game.

Diana looks up to see what's causing the ruckus. "I don't know what the fuck is going on.

I'm just here to show these basketball players what they missing not making me a basketball wife." She says out loud to no one. Rock and Snake overhear her then look at her questionably.

Diana gets to her seat, sits down, then stands up quickly again. "I'm gonna go get some snacks. Maybe I'll catch one of their eyes."

Big Sheddy struggle as he digs into his pocket for money. He grabs a twenty-dollar bill and holds it out toward Diana. "Bring me back a hotdog and a grape pop."

Diana snatches his money. "Nope."

Big Sheddy contemplates going after her but after straining too long to get out of his seat, he just gives up. Diana walks away with an exaggerated swinging of her hips. Rock stares at Diana. When he turns back to look at the game Snake is giving him the eye.

When Diana returns Big Sheddy starts telling her what she missed. Diana hands him his snacks. "Now, Big Sheddy, you know I don't care about nona that shit. Save ya breath."

Rock yells, "Pippen is open, MJ!" Diana plops in her seat and kicks both feet onto the railing in front of them, with her legs wide open, as she eats. She then slowly takes one leg down, seconds apart from each other.

"Aw shit man he didn't see that." Snake says, wiping his forehead. "Rodman open now. Throw it to Rodman, Jordan!" Diana throws both of her feet back onto the railing, with her legs spread apart.

After the referee whistles, Streng yells, "Dat wasn't no got damn fowl." Since he's a few seats away he looks down toward Snake and Rock to yell, "Yall see dat bu'shit!"

Diana places her feet back on the floor.

"I know. He aint even noticing when somebody's wide open!" Rock responds. Diana throws her feet back onto the railing, spreading her legs apart again.

Snake looks puzzled at her. "Da fuck is you doing? Yo ass itching or somethin'? Just scratch it instead of tryna play it off throwin' yo' legs up."

"Yall keep saying Jordan is looking for an open so I'm giving him one," Diana says with that aint-it-obvious look on her face. "Why else he got his tongue hanging out?"

Snake looks disgusted. Rock smiles then shakes his head in disbelief.

The Bulls win another game. The energy is high as the crowd exits the stadium.

Before going to their cars Snake and the others stop in the parking lot to talk. "So, we meeting at Brother's Palace tonight?" Rock asks. Everyone agrees in various forms, even the kids.

Snake jerks his head back, and grunts as his eyes swivel back and forth from Tawny to Tyler. "Ha! Yall wish," Snake says.

Sli playfully pushes Bryk's head. Snake bounces around as if preparing to box. He lightly punches Tyler in the stomach. Tyler grabs his stomach, distorts his face and falls to his knees feigning hurt. They all laugh.

Snake addresses Rock. "Nigga you betta have aaalll the fun you can 'cause it's about to be a wrap for yo' black ugly ass." Snake stares at Rock. "So, you really gon' be somebody's *husband*," Snake says, half asking half stating. He shakes his head, answering his own question. "Naw! You aint ready for that shit."

Rock jerks his head back. "Maaan, aint nothin' gon' be different. We already livin' together."

Snake rapidly blinks his eyes as he tilts his head and stares at Rock a few seconds. "Yeah, you gotta say something to sike yo own damn self out. But you know what? It's a big difference from just living together and being locked down by a contract, 'cause that contract is her ticket to keep gettin' paid way after yo' Black ass leave her or this earth. As a matter of fact, she can kill you silently through yo meals or put a voodoo on you while you laying right next to her and suddenly, just like that she becomes a weeping widow, crying all the way to the social security office to collect that survivor's annuity on yo' behalf, and none would be the wisest. Without that contract she knows she aint gettin' a dime after you die. That's why she gon' act right til them papers get signed."

Everyone laughs. Streng's laughter drowns them all out and lingers even after everyone else has stopped. They all stare at him.

Snake puts his hands together in front of him as if they are in handcuffs. Then changes his voice into a deep guttural tone. "Clink-clink. Looocked…doooown." Everyone laughs.

LATER THAT NIGHT AT BROTHER'S PALACE NIGHT CLUB

Love's gonna last
Love's gonna last
Love's gonna last
Love's gonna last forever
Some people talkin' 'bout you're leaving me here, oh no
Tell me darlin' that they're just teasin' me dear
There are so many things that I've got to do for you
Hey, hey, hey, and if you let me darlin' I'm going to
Make our love last always
Did you hear me baby? Oohoo
Make our love last, always, always…

The song "Love's Gonna Last" by Jeffree is blasting through the club's speakers. People are steppin' on the dance floor. Snake, Felanie and Big Sheddy are sitting at the bar drinking. Sli and Rock are dancing together. Streng is steppin' with an unknown female and Diana is steppin' with an unknown male.

Streng steps out a bit wider than necessary, and accidentally steps on a man's shoe. The man stops dancing to look down at his shoe. "Damn, man!" The man says before shoving Streng, who bumps into Diana, who stumbles backward and falls on her butt. The music stops.

Streng looks behind him to see Diana on the floor then quickly turns to look back at the man. "Wha da fuuu!" Streng says.

Rock and Sli run over to help Diana up.

The man gets in Streng's face. "Nigga you stepped on my gators!"

"Man…my ba'!" Streng says.

"You damn straight it's yo bad but now it's gon' be mo' like yo ass!

"Aw hell! Streng dumb ass done fucked something else up again. I shol aint feeling up to no uninhabited rigmarole right now," Felanie says as she slids down from the bar stool.

Rock, Sli and Diana walk over to stand next to Streng. Big Sheddy, Felanie and Snake shove their way through the crowd to stand next to Streng. Rock slightly slides one side of his jacket back so that the disgruntled gator shoes wearing man notices his gun.

The man tenses up upon seeing it. He looks at Rock, then at the two huge bouncers, who walk up looking like tattooed murderers, who just escaped from prison. One yells out, "Hey!

Yall take that shit outside!" The DJ begins playing the song "People Make the World Go Round" by the Stylistics plays in a low volume.

Streng grins when he sees the man is terrified. Naw man…it's all goo'," Streng tells the bouncers. He turns toward the man and arrogantly asks, "We Coo'?" The man walks away angrily.

As the crowd is dispersing the DJ blasts the Stylistics song.

> *But that's what makes the world go round*
> *The ups and downs, the carousel*
> *Changing people's heads around*
> *Go underground, young man*
> *People make the world go round…*

CHAPTER 7

ROCK'S WEDDING DAY

I ain't no joke. I used to let the mic smoke
Now I slam when I'm done and make sure it's broke
When I'm gone no one gets on cuz I won't let
Nobody press up and mess the seen I set...

The song "I Aint No Joke" by Eric B. is blasting on the stereo in Sli's basement apartment. She lotions her feet before dressing. All the bride's maids will be wearing a satin, fitted lavender mini dress with lavender stilettos. Sli added lavender fish net stockings to her attire. She sprays on perfume. Grabs her mini lavender purse with the long gold link chain and looks at herself in a full-length mirror.

She opens the door, about to leave out, but looks at her wrist and notices she forgot her jewelry. She walks back to her bedroom to look in her jewelry drawer. There is an empty box, with the words Holland's Jewelry. Her mind flashes to her diamond watch and bracelet, which is now missing, then to Tawny's face.

She frantically looks in different places. Opening her closet door, she stares at a large empty box, lying on its side, which was once filled with fireworks. But now there are loose fireworks scattered on the floor.

She pushes clothes over to reveal the back of the closet where a fire safe sits on the floor. She's about to unlock it but notices the safe is already slightly opened. She opens it slowly and sees it is completely empty.

She lets out a scream of frustration, then frantically paces back and forth, before stopping to glare into the full-length mirror, watching her own face grimace with anger. She instantly becomes calm, then lifts her mattress. Inside the box spring, she uncovers a concealed opening to retrieve a metal box. She unlocks it, takes out a handgun, then checks to make sure there are bullets in the chamber before shoving it into her purse.

There is a knock at the door. Sli opens it. Diana walks in dressed in attire like Sli's.

"Uh oooh check you out!" Diana says, grinning while glancing over Sli from head to toe. "Why yo dress shorter than mine?" Diana asks as she lifts her own dress, looking down at herself to see how she'd look in a shorter dress.

"'Cause this how I wanted it." Sli says.

"Oh, okay so you do know that's more like a bare-coo-mini? Diana asks. "What the fuck is you talkin' 'bout?" Sli asks.

"I call it a bare-coo-mini 'cause that skirt barely cover yo coochie. Now you know mama gon' talk aboutchu."

Sli rolls her eyes. "I don't give a fuck. Whatchu want?" "Oh…well damn! You gotta another pair of those fishnets?"

Sli is dazedly staring as she points toward the bedroom. Diana looks at her with a crinkled face.

"Check my stocking drawer." Sli says as she follows Diana into her bedroom.

Diana rummages through the drawer. "Aint no fishnets in here." Diana says as she sits on Sli's bed to put on a tan colored pair of sheer stockings. Diana notices Sli is still staring off blankly. "What's wrong with you?"

Sli quickly turns her head in Diana's direction. "Did you take my jewelry," Sli asks. "What? Nooo! I got my own jewelry." Diana lifts her necklace for emphasis then stands to model-walk around. She stops to stare into the full-length mirror, admiring herself. "Can't nobody tell me shit!" Diana says, adjusting her stockings. As she walks toward the door to leave out, she yells behind her. "Mama almost ready so you can come on out to the car!"

MT. HOOD MISSIONARY BAPTIST CHURCH

Various R&B slow jams and love songs are playing through the wall mounted speakers as guests wait for the wedding to begin.

An hour passes and the wedding still hasn't started. People are restless and looking irritated. Some are leaving. An elderly lady is speaking in a normal conversational tone, but her voice resonates throughout the rows of seats, "Maybe the wedding been cancelled and they just aint told us nothin'."

Two hours have passed, more seats are empty, and more people are leaving. Some people look so worn out as if they've already partied at a reception. A man gets up to leave but not before giving his opinion, "Man…I'm used to CP time, but this done went beyond that. Who *does* this type of shit at they own wedding? This church must not be charging they asses. I betchu they won't be pulling this shit at they funeral though." People laugh.

Three hours later, the wedding finally begins. The people who have remained are looking frustrated. Someone, eating a sandwich, takes a quick bite then hurries to wrap it up. A mother, who is changing her baby's diaper on the pew, begins speeding up the process.

A musical interlude plays before the singer starts.

Oooo oooo whooo
Forever, forever, forever
So, you're having my baby
And it means so much to me
There's nothing more precious
Than to raise a family
If there's any doubt in your mind
You can count on me
I'll never let you down
Lady, believe in me
You and I
Will never fall apart

You and I
We knew right from the start, baby, baby
The day
We fell so far in love
Now our baby is born, healthy and strong
Now our dreams are reality
Forever my lady
It's like a dream
I'm holding you close
You're keeping me warm
If this is ecstasy...

The song "Forever My Lady" by Jodeci plays as each bridesmaid is marching in alongside a groomsman, performing their own variations of sensuous hip swinging and dipping movements, as they march toward the front of the church.

By the time the song ends they are all standing in front of the church's pulpit. The organist hits keys on his organ as an indication that the bride is about to come out. The officiating pastor stands and raises his arms to get everyone in the audience to stand. The rustling sound of bodies standing from their seatsreverberates.

A lady, dressed like a bridesmaid, comes hopping through the church doors and down the aisle as she's putting on her shoes. Once both of her shoes are on, she rushes to stand next to the rest of the bridal party. Some people chuckle, while others whisper and shake their heads with scorn.

The organist chords of "Here Comes the Bride" fades out and the song, "If This World Were Mine" by Luther Vandross and Cheryl Lynn begins playing.

Luther Vandross:
Luther Vandross:
If this world were mine
I would place at your feet
All that I own
You've been so good to me
If this world were mine

I'd give you the flowers the birds and the bees
And it'd be your love beside me
That would be all I need
If this world were mine
I'd give you anything

Cheryl Lynn:
If this world were mine
I would make you a king
With wealth untold
You could have anything
If this world were mine

I'd give you each day so sunny and blue
And if you wanted the moonlight
I'd give you that too
If this world were mine, oh, baby
I'd give you anything…

The bride walks extremely slowly, taking tiny steps down the aisle, she even stops a few times to dance in place. People hoot and yell out, egging her on each time. The bride accomplishes her goal to not get to the front of the church until the song is ending. When she stops before the preacher Rock stands beside her.

The preacher says all the necessary things required to complete the ceremony then announces, "You may kiss the bride." Rock kisses his new wife.

Everyone applauds and cheer. The bride and groom walk away waving.

THE CHATEAU BU'SCHE
It's time for the Percolator
It's time for the Percolator
It's time for the Percolator
It's time for the Percolator

The Chicago House Music song "The Percolator" by Curtis Alan Jones is blaring. Some people are on the dance floor. Some are standing in line at the buffet, and several are already eating at their assigned tables.

Those on the dance floor periodically yell out in excitement, egging on the most creative movements of those doing the percolator dance.

Sli is among those cheering the best dancers on. She looks away and spots Tawny going to the bathroom, so she follows her.

Tawny is already in a stall by the time Sli gets to the bathroom, so she looks under each of the stall doors to see where Tawny is. When she recognizes Tawny's shoes, she waits in front of the stall.

When Tawny is coming out Sli grabs Tawny's neck, steering her against the wall of the disabled stall. "You stole from me again." Sli says through gritted teeth. Sli puts her finger to her own lips signaling Tawny to shush. Tawny rapidly shakes her head. Sli harshly slides her feet against the back of Tawny's heels making her slam to the floor, landing next to the toilet.

Sli shoves her hand into her purse and pulls out a gun. She presses it against Tawny's temple. Several hears someone walk into the bathroom. Sli whispers. "We'll finish this discussion later. Or we may not need to if you just bring my shit back. I let you slide once. It won't happen again. If I don't get my shit back, I swear this gon' cost you your life.

Now getcho ass up, smile and act like nona this happened. You got it?" Tawny nods.

They're leaving the bathroom. Sli looks at Tawny's face; her lips are puckered. Sli grabs Tawny's arm. "That's not how yo ass smile." Tawny musters a fake smile.

They walk out and see the family is taking pictures and join them.

CHAPTER 8

In Adisa's Hair Braiding Salon Big Sheddy is sweeping, answering calls, ordering, and stocking various hair care products and supplies while eavesdropping on various conversations. He stops periodically to look up at the television mounted on the wall even though the sound is muted. Reggae music plays from a speaker hanging in a corner next to the television.

There is a customer seated in each of the four swivel chairs getting their hair braided. Sli and Felanie are braiding Nicky's hair together. Sli stops braiding and holds the unfinished braid in one hand as she swings Nicky's chair around to look her in the face, which yanks the braid Felanie is working on from her hand. Felanie throws her hands in the air then places them on her hips. Sli puts her free hand on her waist. "So, wait a minute, Nicky. Hold on…I need to make sure I heardchu properly. Whatchu sayin' is the judge got that much power to the point that she can determine *where* the criminals do their time…regardless of where the crime was committed?"

"Girrrlfriend! You heard me right. It aint that easy though." Nicky puts her hand out to point to each finger as she names a title. "'Cause she needs other cops, doctors, psychiatrists, psychologists, attorneys, whoever… And hell sometimes, even the pegged criminal's own damn mammy and pappy to agree to sign fake proof that the criminal was wherever they decide they wanna put them. And you best believe they gettin' paid real good enough to get those lies documented, certified and notarized. They got mufukas in er' country helpin' they asses with that shit. If they don't like a mufuka he gets fucked big time. But they usually do that to those big wigs who get caught or confess to doin' dumb shit." Nicky jerks her heard. "Now what I don't get is why do white people confess to anythang, especially since they already know their fellow lying ass clansman would get them out of anything, long as they continue to deny it. 'Cause whenever they admit to being guilty that pisses their clans' friends the hell off. And they don't give a flying fuck if it *is* on camera. They can still get them off. All they gotta do is fake remorse and show phony tears and keep lying and denying. They gon' pay big to get they own out of whatever shit they did, especially if it was done to one of our Black asses. ALL they white asses aint nothin' but undercover crooks. It's a whole conglomerate of corporate and government mafia muthufuckas. You hear me?"

"Daaaamn, giiirl that's some wild shit!" Sli goes back to braiding Nicky's hair. Felanie grabs the one she was working and continues braiding it.

"Girrrlfriend! Naw what's wild is watchin' those upstanding grown ass white men break down cryin' in the courthouse like li' bitches when the judge yells: "TEN YEARS IN THE CUBAN PENETENTIARY." And all they asses know damn well aint none of 'em been nowhere near no damned South America." Sli and Nicky laugh, Felanie shakes her head.

"I wanna snitch so bad but it's this one fine ass buff chocolate attorney on their teamwho I want to fuck the shit outta me first. But girrrlfriend, I'm working on convincing him how bad he wants me too 'cause he still don't know it yet." Again, Sli and Nicky burst out laughing, Felanie chuckles.

Nicky looks up from laughing to lock eyes and wink at Big Sheddy. Big Sheddy stops sweeping. He looks stunned but feels confusedly flattered.

The bells over the door jingle when a man walks in with an oversized duffel bag. He looks like he fell on hard times—unkempt facial hair and wearing layers of untidy and oversized attire.

Once the door shuts, the man hurriedly puts the bag on the floor to pull out women's shoes, thigh high boots, purses, towels, jewelry, and other paraphernalia. He looks up and smiles to reveal sporadic missing teeth before standing again. He limps through the shop with a few items in his hands, and some dangling across his arms and shoulders. Everyone's head turns toward him.

Fresh off the freight, so you know it's great!
My name is Cooper, but you can call me Coop.
Accessories: from bangles, bags to boots.
Got toys for yo' kids that can spin, sang, or shoot.
Wanna eat?
Got those sour, sugary, and salty treats.
Need something at home?
Check out my cutlery, candles, brushes and combs.
If you need it, and I don't got it, just let it be known.
I'll cop it when I can. I SWEAR the wait won't be long.
Be back here in a flash; sangin' this same ole song.

Cooper stops to stare at Nicky. Nicky stares at the items he's holding. "Them some badass thigh high boots," Nicky says. How much you want for 'em?"

"Whatchu think they worth?" Cooper asks.

"See I hate when mufukas ask me crazy ass questions 'cause I give crazy ass answers." Nicky says rolling her eyes. "Gray the only color you got?"

"What color you want?"

Nicky puckers her lips, lifting her eyebrows before responding. "Red."

Cooper rolls his eyes and lets out a long sigh. "Now had I had red you would've wanted them to be orange, or yellow or raaainbow or some shit."

Nicky jerks her head back. "Ooo...Uh...Yeah well if yo' shyster ass would've been a real businessman you would've had every fucking color in the Crayola box."

Cooper looks at Nicky sideways. "Well damn you sho move quick! Didn't I just see you standing out there on Madison?"

"Now I know damn well me and yo mama don't look *nothin'* alike."

"Well, you sho right 'bout that cause my mama aint never looked like no booger wolf." Cooper agrees raising his eyebrows.

"Well now speaking of yo mama I sho hope you took time to thank her." Everybody looks at Nicky with confusion. "Cause I can only imagine how hard it must have been for her *not* to eat you at birth with you being her only defected, ugly ass litter." They all laugh, even Cooper chuckles as he limps back to his bag to put the items backinside.

"Boooi, yall faggots sho be quick with that wit." Cooper finally says.

"Oh, I got yo faggot. It's a wonder yo old bald mouth ass aint choked to death yet since you gotta swallow yo food whole."

Cooper looks up at Nicky, shakes his head, and continues packing his things. He hoists the bag on his shoulder and limps toward the door.

"A'ight yall have a good day. See you back out here on the strip in a few, Ms. Madison Street walker." Cooper salutes and grins, this time without his lips parting.

Nicky looks stunned, glancing quickly around the room. "Nooo… that nigga didn't just call me a Madison Street walker! Yeah, well you'll definitely know it's me mufucka 'cause I'll be standin right next to yo funky tale mammy! That's right limp yo old stankin' ass on up outta here. Lookin' like Kunta Kinte on crack."

Cooper walks out the door sticking up his middle finger. Big Sheddy walks behind him, locking the door.

Sli starts in. "Da fuck Big Sheddy! Yo ass is slippin'…*again*! Man, you can't be doin' that shit on Madison Street, especially at this time a day! Glad Ms. Adisa aint here or we all would've had to hear her mouth. And listen here, Ms. Nicky, you need to watch that smart-ass mouth. Mufukas be packin'. And with that big ass bag he had, it could've easily held an Uzi in that bitch."

"Girrrlfriend! Do I look like I was worried 'bout that nigga? If anythang he needs to be worried 'bout me."

CHAPTER 9

Tupac's song, "Keep Ya Head Up," is blasting from a car's stereo.

Fresh off the freight, so you know it's great!
My name is Cooper, but you can call me Coop.
Accessories: from bangles, bags to boots.
Got toys for yo' kids that can spin, sang, or shoot.
Wanna eat?
Got those sour, sugary, and salty treats.
Need something at home?
Check out my cutlery, candles, brushes and combs.
If you need it, and I don't got it, just let it be known.
I'll cop it when I can. I SWEAR the wait won't be long.
Be back here in a flash; sangin' this same ole song.
Time to heal our women, be real to our women
And if we don't we'll have a race of babies
That will hate the ladies, that make the babies
And since a man can't make one
He has no right to tell a woman when and where to create one
So will the real men get up
I know you're fed-up ladies, but keep your head up

Keep ya head up, oooo child things are gonna get easier
ooooo child things are gonna get brighter...

Rock and Odeo are each repairing vehicles. Snake is in his office typing on the computer, shuffling papers, and talking on the phone. His door is open, but Odeo knocks anyway. Snake beckons for him to have a seat. As he's about to sit, Snake gestures for him to close the door.

Odeo does it, then sits down as he looks around at the various pictures sitting behind Snake's seat, and along the walls. After a few minutes, Snake finally ends the call.

"Give me a few," Snake says. "I need to write all this down, right quick so I won't forget nothin'." When he's finished writing, he leans back in his chair, twirling an ink pen between his fingers, gazing into space, before abruptly acknowledging Odeo. "So what's up O?"

Snake leans forward to insure he understands because Odeo's Hispanic accent makes it challenging. "Yo man ju know I really don't want to boder you with my personal problems but I'm goeng tru a ruf patch wit my money right now. Ju know my lady is about to have our seven babies so you can imagene just how tight tings are at the house. Ya feel me? No?"

"Wait…so you sayin' she's having sextuplets?"

Odeo smacks his lips and rolls his eyes in his head. "No, no, no. Baby numba seven, man."

Snake raises his eyebrows then slowly nods. "Weeeell, Odeo, I do understand. Times can get hard but…"

"Wait!" Odeo interrupts. "Jusss hear me out. I wanna work extra hours each day to earn it so ju worry 'bout nuting. But I need cash right now." Odeo rubs his index and middle fingers against his thumb for emphasis. "Like last week, ju know what I mean? Plus, I was wondereng if ju to give me the next two pay checks right now. No wait, so I catch up on bills?"

Snake grimaces as if mulling it over. "See Odeo I'm doing my own struggling right now, trying to make sure you and Rock get paid, each week, and on time. So, to give you extra money up front is just not doable right now."

Odeo scoots forward in his seat. "Come on maaan. I know ju understand about family. Ju have beautiful one jourself." Odeo points to a picture hanging on the wall behind Snake. "Those jour kids?"

Snake points as he explains who the kids are. "These are my twins, Tawny and Tyler and this is my nephew, Bryk."

"Aw man dey all look just like ju. Even your nephew could be jours. That's amazing." Odeo smiles nodding. "But what I was saying is see it not be like jou're losin' aneeteng. I work extra hours early mornengs, and late evenengs. Be like…ovatime, but wit jus' regular money…No extra money." He uses a finger to point to the fingers on his other hand to emphasize his points. "I do more. Customerrrs get car back fasterrr. Great for business. And everybody's happy. No?"

Snake sits in a daydream like state, a few seconds, before shaking his head. "Sorry Odeo but that would mean I would have to come in earlier to let you in and stay later to lock up…"

"Come on maaan." Odeo gets loud, shaking his head and throwing his hands in the air. "No ju won't. I do all myself."

"Naw man, sorry. I'm not ready for all that, and I don't have the funds readily available anyway. Wish I did."

Odeo sits back, disappointed. A customer knocks on the door. Snake yells come in. The customer steps into Snake's office and is surprised to see someone else is sitting down.

Odeo stands then aggressively sticks his hand into the candy jar and pulls out a fist full of candies. Some fall onto the desk, leaving only a few in the jar. He then grabs half the ink pens displaying the company's information on them before finally walking out.

Snake is about to snap but remembers the visitor is watching. "What's up Brandon! We were just finishing up in here. Come on in. Have a seat. It's good to see you again especially since you're one of our faithful, no haggling customers. Since you haven't been here in a while that could only mean we did a hell of job with repairing that fine Lexus of yours. Unless you cheatin' on us and fell in love with another repair place."

"Yeah, well that fine Lexus needs repairing again. It keeps cutting off on me at random times. I gotta represent a client this afternoon and didn't want to take a chance driving it, and either be late or not getting there at all."

"So, it sounds like you're still representing the guilty huh?" Snake chuckles.

Brandon looks at him sideways. "You better be careful how you judging folks. That may just be you crying in handcuffs someday."

"Naw man. I go the extra mile to keep my nose clean." Snake holds his head up to display his nostrils. "See not a mess found. ALL CLEAR!"

They both laugh. Then Brandon gets a serious look. "But man, I'm telling you…some of the stuff that happens in that courthouse will shock you. You know it's scary how…Naw man…You know what…I didn't come here for this…"

"Hold on now. This stuff can wait. What's goin on man?"

Brandon slowly shakes his head. "Our justice system is filled with nothing but legalized crooks, walking around here free, every day, and will probably never know what it's like to pay for their own mess."

"Aw man I thought you was about to tell me some outlandish shit!" Snake stands to step away from his desk. "Yeah, well on that note I do have to get back to work."

"Naw man hear me out." Snake sits back down as Brandon continues. "I love being an attorney, but it's starting to fuck with me. The judge is sending folks to jail in countries they've never even heard of, let alone actually been to."

"And what that gotta do with you?"

"The judge is making us conjure up fake records as proof that those who are perceived as guilty were in certain countries, at particular times and days."

"*Making* you?" Snake blurts. "Sounds like you makin' a lotta extra loot being involved with shit like that."

"Well, I can't say I am, but those foreign prison owners are paying a lotta loot to somebody to keep their spots running 'cause you know most of them are in poor countries. They make those prisoners work they asses off. It's basically free labor in like a legal…" Brandon throws up air quotes. "…twisted form of human trafficking." Brandon sits back flustered. "Man, what else am I supposed to do? I need to eat and keep a crib. Plus, basic maintenance aint cheap." Brandon points toward his car. Leaning forward, he scratches his bald head, then excessively wipes his head and face with both hands.

"Well, whatchu gon' do?" Snake asks.

Brandon sits back again and waits a few seconds before responding. "I don't know. I'll have to deal with it for now. So, can I get a rental?"

"A rental?" Snake chuckles. "You musta forgot where the fuck you at."

"Naw man I figured you gotta hoopty, or some trap you can loan me that's guaranteed to, at least, get me to my next location and back til…"

Snake tilts his head and twists lip.

Brandon raises his eyebrows. "Yeah, yeah. Okay. I'll grab a cab, or bus, maybe even a bike or something. Call me as soon as you know the damages."

"Of course." They both stand. Brandon walks out.

Odeo, who is standing nearby, wiping his hands on a towel heard their conversation and is staring at Brandon as he leaves.

****

Later that evening Snake is processing paperwork from business transactions made throughout the day. He makes a call to Brandon. "Hey man! Listen…we found what's wrong with your vehicle. It's a strange area that's not quite the engine but it plays a major part helping it function right. And by your vehicle being a foreign classic it's a challenge finding the part you need. Actually, it's more like a combination of parts needed to get it functioning again. You know what I'm sayin'. I've been calling around to different places looking for parts but they either have the correct parts for the wrong year or they have only the one part for the right year but not that other part we need. Yea…uh huh…Correct."

Snake is doodling but stops to lean back as he continues listening to Brandon. "Yep.

Okay so now the options are if you're willing to wait it out, I can order them from overseas but that would mean having to wait a couple of weeks or maybe even longer. Or you can take your chances and we can just go with that one part. But if you do that, you're risking it breaking down again. Then you'll be right back in here maybe days or even weeks later. But you never know it may be all you need to keep it running right for a li' while. It's a risk. Or if you don't wanna do anything with it right now you can just come back in to pick it up. I'll hang around for a few 'cause I can nigger rig it so it's guaranteed to get you back to where you need to be without it cutting off on you…You know what I mean, but anything after that is all on you. Okay…cool.

I'll go ahead and order those parts and let you know when they finally get here. Okay talk to you soon." Snake hangs up and finishes up in the office before leaving for the evening.

CHAPTER 10

Haddie closes the outside door and is about to descend the steps but stops to feel around inside her purse. Diana walks up with shopping bags in her hands. She stops at the bottom of the steps. "Ma, where you going? Looking all jazzy."

Haddie continues looking in her purse. "The beat meeting."

"Okay wait for me. I'm goin' withchu. Just let me put my bags up. How you like my new outfit? When Haddie looks up from her purse to stare at Diana, her mouth slowly opens.

"What?" Diana looks behind her to see if Haddie is looking at something else. "You looking behind me or gawking at my sexy self?" Diana asks turning around, displaying her entire sheer outfit but looking more like she's seducing herself. "I got it off the clearance rack."

Haddie tightens her lips, while rolling her eyes and head. "And do you know why it was on Clearance?"

Diana's eyebrows crinkles and her lips twist. She opens her mouth to respond.

Haddie cuts her off. "'Cause er'body can see clear straight to the crack of yo' tits and ass.

You look stanky, girl. You aint going nowhere with me with that on."

Diana opens the gate then runs upstairs. "Come on ma. Even you know people are blessed when they see all this sexiness. I didn't buy this to just sit in the house, and since I have nowhere else to go right now, the beat meeting'll work."

Haddie, walking downstairs, yells out. "Can't you just sit yo ass in the window like you do when you aint got nowhere to go, but still paint yo face?"

Diana drops her shopping bags on the inside steps to their apartment then runs back outside. "Come on now ma! You know that aint gonna work with this outfit! I need to be standing as much as possible for people to get the full affect."

Haddie opens the car door, then looks up to see Diana walking toward her still wearing the same outfit. Haddie is clearly frustrated. Diana looks back at her then quickly plasters a cheesy tight grin across her lips as she gets into the car.

"So, you really just don't care how stanky you look right now?" Haddie asks.

"Ma! Stop playin'. You just done got too old to recognize what real sexiness is. You forgot how back in yo' day you thought them ugly bouffant hairdos, looking like a George Washington wig, and corsets, and barrel shaped dresses, with those fake booty draws underneath was sexy. And I'm sure yo mama said you looked stanky too, but that didn't make you go and snatch yo' stuff off…Now did it? Nope"

Haddie looks at her confused, opens her mouth to say something but closes it again. She opens her mouth again but nothing comes out right away. "First of all, the barrel shaped dresses are called crinolines, and second of all that was like a thousand years before I was even thought of." Haddie shakes her head and giggles, as she drives away.

CHAPTER 11

Several people are shouting in discontent. There is a panel of men and women who hold positions as beat captain, alderman, precinct captain, ward members and their assistants sitting at a rectangular table, in front of an audience. The beat captain yells out, "I'm gonna need everyone to calm down!" The voices trickle down to whispers.

A man stands up to speak. "That's the problem we've already been too calm long enough! It's not enough that nothing is being done to control the thugs and gangs, but we can't even get sufficient street, or even traffic lights! And I'm not even gonna get started on the dangerous potholes that goes for miles long down our streets!"

The beat captain holds his hand up. "This is what I'm trying to explain to you all. All the paperwork has been turned in and you all know how the red tape with any government works, especially in Chicago."

Haddie raises her hand.

"Go ahead Ms. Haddie," the beat captain acknowledges.

"I think I have a solution," Haddie says. "Perhaps I can help speed things up."

"How so?"

"See, I had the privilege of attending an African ritual, where they chant words to help speed certain life processes along. But first let me ask all of you on the panel. In the neighborhoods where you live, is there sufficient streetlights at night?"

A few panel members nod their heads. Some say yes.

"And I'm also sure the streets in your neighborhoods are *not* covered in holes so big that it could swallow an entire semi-tractor trailer truck. Correct?"

Certain panel members agree again. Some are not responding because they are aware she's setting them up.

"Of course, as I figured," Haddie continues. "And all we want is that same neighborhood niceness. Okay, so, now that you understand, there's an African chant I'd like all of us to do.

According to this ritual, we can be granted the same luxury in life as those who claim to be our leaders, if we chant these words…wait… how does it go now?" Haddie rubs her finger across her chin, tilting her head toward the ceiling. "Oh yeah…So da fa duwe," she says slowly, then a bit faster the second time. "So, da fa duwe." She turns toward the audience to get them to join in. "Come on chant with me yall."

Everyone starts chanting, "so da fa duwe." Haddie makes it clear what she's really saying to Diana. Diana looks shocked and bursts up laughing. Haddie turns to the person on the other side of her, then bends down to say it in the ear of the person in front of her. She turns to face the man sitting behind her. Diana and others pass it along. Everyone begins catching on.

SO THE FUCK DO WE!
SO THE FUCK DO WE!
SO THE FUCK DO WE!

Some panel members are outraged, some are looking defeated, while some are smiling and bobbing their heads to the beat of the chant.

****

The meeting ends and Haddie and Diana are walking to the car. "Can we stop to get some catfish and scrimps?" Diana asks.

"Excuse me, Madam Haddie."

Haddie and Diana turn to see who is talking.

"My name is Theodore Cooper Goins, but I prefer being called Ted, or even like a cuddly bear, Teddy if *you* choose." Ted smiles.

"I'll keep that in mind. Well, you can just call me Haddie. Lose the Madam part." Ted extends his hand. They shake. "Whatever *you* desire Queen Haddie."

"You gots to be Madam Haddie's, I mean, Haddie's sister." Diana chuckles. Haddie interjects. "She's my daughter, Diana."

"Pleased to meet you. I don't want to take up too much of your time. I just wanted to let you know I enjoyed your speech this evening."

Haddie and Diana chuckle. "Why thank you, Ted. I'm glad you enjoyed it. I'm sure the panel would totally disagree with you. And I'm positive they hope I never show up here again." Haddie says, chuckling. "And I'd hardly call it a speech. It felt more like a performance."

"Leave it to Mama." Diana blurts, while shaking her head.

Haddie and Ted look at Diana, as if they forgot she was standing there. Diana looks back and forth at them. "Yeeeah…Uuum…Give me yo' keys, Ma. I'll go start the car," Diana says, then walks away.

"I was hoping, you and I could discuss more about the neighborhood improvements over a cup of coffee. Or are you into tea?" Ted asks.

"That may just work for me. I'm into both." Haddie says.

Ted goes into his pocket, retrieving a pen, and a torn piece of paper, he holds it toward Haddie. "I'll need your number."

Haddie writes her number on the paper.

"Is it okay if I walk you to your car?" Ted asks. "Of course."

When they arrive at Haddie's car, Ted opens the door. Haddie gets in.

"I'm going to tell you like my mom always tell me…" Ted changes his voice to sound like an elderly woman. "You have to drive for yourself and er'body else out there."

Haddie smiles. "I certainly agree with that."

"Sooo, *you* be sure to stay safe out here, Haddie. So, you can be available to hear from me real soon."

"Looking forward to it. And you stay safe out here as well," Haddie tells him.

Ted says, Talk to you soon," at the same time as Haddie says, "Talk to you later." They both smile.

"Bye now." Ted says before closing the car door.

Haddie drives off. "So ma, you out here tryna find us a new daddy?"

"Girl hush. Probably just another greasy nigga from Greasy Corner, Arkansas." They both burst out laughing. Diana shakes her head.

"Un un. Dontchu start! See Ma, you just aint ever gon' be right is you."

****

Ted and Haddie talk regularly on the phone. Eventually they begin dating. They go to various places throughout the months:

- A live screenplay performance, at a musical theater where dinner isserved.
- The House of Blues for dinner, and a liveband.
- Ted drops Haddie off at home. He walks her to the front door. They are kissing, when Snake interrupts them, when he opens the front door, and stares at Ted. Haddie introduces Ted to Snake. They shake hands. Ted awkwardly walks off wavinggoodbye
- Ted and Haddie are at the Taste of Chicago, feeding each other samples ofdishes, watching live stage performances, as they walk along, holdinghands.
- Ted cooks dinner for Haddie. After dinner they watch a movie, drink wine and make love.

CHAPTER 12

Customers are getting their hair braided. Music and various conversations fill the shop.

Big Sheddy is busying himself around the shop, sweeping, answering calls, ordering, and stocking various hair care products and supplies, while eaves dropping as usual.

Sli and Felanie are braiding Nicky's hair as she thumbs through a magazine. She slams the magazine down in her lap. "Girrrlfriend! Now that my hormone treatments are almost over and I can finally afford to pay to become a full-blown fucking *woman,* a bitch don't know how to act." Nicky snaps her fingers in a Z formation.

"Sooo whatchu you sayin'?" Sli asks. "I'm getting it chopped the hell off."

Along with their bottom lips, Sli and Felanie drop the extensions they were braiding. Felanie slowly side steps until she is standing directly in front of Nicky. "Wait! Sooo, you're actually getting yo' dick cut off?

"Yaaaaasss bitches!" Nicky lets out an ear-piercing scream, is gyrating in her seat and waving her arms and the magazine in the air. "I'm getting a whole new vagina!!!"

Everybody stops talking and looks in Nicky's direction. Nicky looks back at everyone. The music stops playing but that's because it has ended. A different song begins playing. Nicky contains herself long enough to go back to thumbing through the magazine. "I waited long enough, shiiiit!" Nicky softly says to herself.

Again, unable to contain her excitement, Nicky closes the magazine. "Don't yall wanna know how it's done?"

Sli and Felanie look confused because they don't know how to respond. Sli shakes her head as Felanie nods.

"I think I kind of got the idea," Felanie says.

"I'm sure you don't even," Nicky blurts. "Okay, okay yall listen up. It's quite a fascinating process." Nicky says as she throws her hands and arms around. "Once they castrate my testicles, they take the loose skin and the dick and push it inside me to make a flap and the clitoris. That way the nerves and blood can connect and flow properly. And hopefully there's enough skin 'cause my doctor said if there's not enough skin, they would have to take a graft from my thighs and hips. But I'm pretty sure they aint gon' have that to wor' bout. You know what I mean." Nicky laughs with her lips and teeth quivering excessively.

Big Sheddy runs to the trash bin and vomits. Everyone looks at Big Sheddy frowning. "You okay Big Sheddy?" Sli asks laughing.

Nicky rolls her eyes. "Intyway…Girrrlfriend! You know I aint having them cutting nothing extra…skin graft, near or around this voluptuous booty? I think not. These hips and thighs must be smooth and scar free at all costs. Can't be on no beach looking like I wasclawed by my neighbor's mangy ass cats. A bitch gots to be flawless. Ugly bitches can't make as much money as Ido."

Felanie scratches her chin. "Hmmm…this is interesting. So, I've been contemplating something else you may want to seriously consider. Even though a dick *can* get malodorous, and a pussy can get all types of ways of putrid, I highly doubt you'll have the genuine reeky coochie smell, with yours about to be brand new and all, especially if aint been penetrated yet. So, you gonna need to bottle some various decayed coochie scents to convince yo tricks you legit. Ya heard?"

Nicky and Sli cut their eyes at Felanie.

Sli is parting Nicky's hair then drops her hand to her thigh. "I keep telling you yo' ass is crazy, and you just keep proving me right." Sli says to Felanie.

"Naw, naw now hear me out. *You* can profit from this too, Sli," Felanie assures. "See Nicky's gonna need the repulsiveness of early morning skunky pussy, after it's been simmering all night; midafternoon putrid pussy; evening rancid pussy; no shower all day rank pussy; evening decomposing pussy." Felanie squints her eyes, contemplating before asking, "Am I missing something?"

Sli and Nicky shake their heads until Sli has a second thought. "But hold on. I don't know how you figure I can help with that. You make pussy sound like it smells worse than a decomposed body. And my shit aint nothin' like how you make it sound."

"Don't forget the bleeding period *revolting* pussy smell 'cause I definitely can't do that one." Nicky adds.

"I got something especially for that." Felanie says as she reaches into the bottom drawer of the vanity desk to pull out a bag. The shop's phone begins ringing.

"You gotta call, Felanie!" Big Sheddy yells.

"Damn! Who is this interrupting my flow?" Felanie says as she walks away. "Something is seriously wrong with yo' friend." Nicky whispers.

"Girl I keep reminding her that most people do have some loose screws, but that crazy bitch got hers jiggling around inside her head. And I swear sometimes I can even see them poking out her ears." Nicky and Sli are laughing when Felanie returns.

"You gon' be available Saturday morning?" Felanie asks. "Why?" Sli asks.

"Ms. Banie wanna bring the twins at 6:00 in the morning." "Damn why so early?" Sli asks.

"That's not my business. Yes, or no?" "I guess so.

"Sli please don't have me in here by myself again doing both of their heads." "I said Okay…Damn."

Felanie runs back to the phone, returning seconds later. "Now check these out." Felanie says as she holds out plastic vials. "This one's for those who bleed for only three days. This one is for the five-day bleeder, and this is for the seven dayers."

Sli and Nicky are gazing with their mouths opened.

Felanie continues explaining. "This fancy doodad here helps clot the blood for if you really want to convince him you got fibroid tumors and cysts on yo ovaries and shit like that. You know like that Fibromyalgia, and PMS type bullshit. But what would really get him is if you pour the blood and a few clots on his sheets while he's sleeping. That nigga will never suspect you ever had a dick like him. And nobody would be able to convince himotherwise."

Everyone is awkwardly quiet for a few seconds before Sli decides to break the tension. "How about the after fucking, pissing and shitting stanky pussy?"

"Naw she won't need that in a vial." Felanie says.

"Naw. I will have *that* one down pat myself." Nicky says. "True dat. Dat you will." Sli says. They all nod.

"Well now there's still the after eating certain foods scents cause he's gonna wanna lick it fo he sticks it. Might as well keep him well nourished. So, you'll need the after eating soul food scented pussy, salad or even McDonald's and Burger King scents." Felanie continues.

Sli stops braiding to look at Felanie and put her hands on her hips. "And just how are you planning to make this shit happen, Felanie?" Sli goes back to braiding Nicky's hair.

"Easy. You eat those type of foods you want to pass on through the coochie juices, wait a half hour to an hour for it all to digest and voila" Felanie pulls from her bag a life like rubber snake and an empty bottle with a cheesecloth rubber banded over the top of it.

Sli and Nicky recoil. Someone, looking from across the room yells, "Da fuck!"

"You ever seen how they milk the poison from a snake's mouth?" No one responds.

Felanie continues, using here props to demonstrate. "They push the snake's fangs into a cheesecloth that's rubber banded on top of a jar, smashing its open mouth down so that all of its venom drains into the jar and the unneeded impurities stay on top of the cheesecloth. We can do it the same way with coochie juices. So just in case the chic has the crabs or some shit then the cheesecloth will catch that shit. Or maybe not but that's the plan." Felanie chuckles. "Anyway, with enough of us contributing daily, we should have an entire distribution running in 72months. I can see it now..." Felanie places her hands in the air as if posting a sign, the rubber snake's lower body wiggles uncontrollably. "Felanie's Funky Kuchy Kreamatory." She drops her arms down, gazing at her spectators. "Kuchy gots be spelled k-u-c-h-y though so dumb mufukas would have to come in and ask what that is? 'Cause yall already know those Kush heads coming in looking to get high will be pronouncing it wrong. And that's 'cause not only could they assess not spell but they lack the pertinent knowledge to know how to phonetically pronounce or spell words they've never seen before. They don't know that c-h is not pronounced sh, except in certain instances. The only one I can think of now is how some mamas spell their child's names differently, like Cheryl can be spelled s-h or c-h. Just like Kreamatory will be spelled with a k too but it's referring to cream as in the goop that comes out the coochie, not the burial site. So, check it…they gone come inside the factory asking about that Kush, thinking it's weed,right.

And we gone either make a pitch for them to donate they pussy juice, if they're females, and if they're dudes then we give them a pamphlet for referrals. Once they see they're getting two dollara a pop for a whole vial, they're going to run and tell they're mamas, wives, sisters, aunties, baby mamas and even they grannies shiiiiit. "'Cause the weed heads know they're getting a cut too." Felanie steps back and throws her hands in the air as if she scored a touchdown. "It's a win-win baby! Business gone be booming yall!" Felanie sees everyone has a nonchalant look on their faces, which discourages her. "If yall act right," she says.

Nicky and Sli give Felanie a twisted look.

Sli turns her head and asks, "If you're payin' them two dollars to donate, how much you selling the vials for?"

"Now that depends upon the market. It's all about supply and demand. With more sells I can keep the price down and vice versa." Felanie says as she humps her shoulders.

Nicky bursts up laughing. "Well now not only am I convinced that this is the most lunatic type shit I've ever heard, but it's obvious that you *could not* have *just* come up with this entire bullshit. This something you've apparently been working out for too damn long. Chile you need a newlife."

Felanie is staring off, nodding and smiling with pride.

CHAPTER 13

Ted and Haddie are at Dusty's Soul Food Restaurant. Their plates are loaded with food they've piled on at the buffet as they slide into a booth, sitting across from each other. Ted rubs his hands together slowly before speaking. "Haddie, I want to know everything about you."

"Well, now I highly doubt we have time for me to tell you *everything* tonight." "Oooh, you got somewhere more important you need to be tonight?" Ted says with a grin.

Haddie smiles back. "As a matter of fact, I do...Like trying to get a good night's sleep."

Ted raises his eyebrows as he nods. "I can certainly relate to that myself. Which part of the south you from?"

Haddie raises her eyebrows. "It's that obvious huh? I'm from Tupelo, Mississippi. Been married and divorced once. Got three kids: a boy and girl twins and you met my baby girl, Diana." Haddie pauses, staring at the saltshaker, contemplating what else she should disclose. "I own a duplex apartment building where we all live. I have three grand kids: another set of boy and girl twins and a grandson. All teenagers. I retired from the Post Office after thirty years.

And, since I don't have a life, as you already witnessed, I get a kick outta making things happen, even if I have to use a crowd to help me do it."

They both burst out laughing; Ted much louder than he meant to. Haddie takes a sip of her coke. "Now tell me about you."

Ted sips his iced tea. "I retired from IBM as an engineer, after forty years." Haddie jerks her head back. Ted smirks but continues talking as if he'd rehearsed it, specifically for this moment. "Never been married. No kids. Live in the South Suburbs."

Haddie opens her mouth, attempting to speak. Ted puts his hands up. "I know you wondering why am I all the way in over here, in the hood of the wesssiiide!" He holds up his hand with the two middle fingers crossed, and the pinky and index fingers spread to form the letter "W."

Haddie giggles and looks around in embarrassment. Teddy chuckles. "Naw but my mom lives up the street from you. I'm an only child so that leaves only me to help her out."

"Have you looked into home care for her?"

"I've considered it, but she only needs help sporadically throughout certain weeks. Some weeks she won't need help at all. Being that inconsistent doesn't set well with most agencies." Ted shrugs his shoulders. "So, she's stuck with me."

The corners of Haddie's lips turn downward as she nods. "Then that would explain why you attended *our* beat meeting…for yo' Mamma. And what do you do on those days she doesn't need you?"

Ted leans forward, placing his elbows on the table, he clasps his hand under his chin. "I ride my bike aro…"

"May I take those plates?" A waiter interrupts. Ted leans back, feeling relieved.

Another weekend they go bowling. Haddie wins and brags incessantly to Ted and anyone who would listen.

On another date they go stepping at Chic Rick's night club.

Months pass as they continue dating. Ted knew after introducing himself to Haddie, after that beat meeting that she would be his wife. Now he needs to find out if she agrees. But first he has get her son's blessings.

Ted visits Snake at his auto repair shop. Snake is staring at a car parked in front of his shop.

He turns behind him to see Ted walking towards him. "Well hello Mr. Ted. What can I do for you?" Snake asks as he continues writing on his clip board.

"Well, Snake, unfortunately I'm not here to bring you more business. But fortunately, that means my car is running just fine. I hope I'm not interrupting you at a busy time. I need to speak with you about something personal." Ted looks around and notices Rock and Odeo are in ear shot. "Can we talk somewhere private?"

Snake looks at Ted with concern. Ted lays his hand on Snake's shoulder. "Oh no it's nothing to worry about."

"Sure. Step in my office," Snake says as they go into his office. Snake beckons Ted to sit down as he sits behind his desk.

"I'll get straight to the point. You know I knew your mom was someone special when I first laid eyes on her at that beat meeting and I..."

"Yeah, I'd have to agree with ya there." Snake cuts him off. "Apparently, I too have been in love with her since I popped out." Snake tilts his head. "So, you here to tell me you ready to make my mama yo' wife." Snake smiles, Ted smiles back.

"Well now that you've helped me get the hard part out the way what's your answer?"

Snake stands and walks toward the front of his desk to lean his butt against it, where he is close enough to Ted to look him directly in the eyes. "I can tell mama is so much happier since you two've been spendin' time together. I wish yall the best maaan. I will be proud to walk her down the aisle and give her to you."

Ted stands. They hug. "I appreciate this man. Imma take damn good care of your mom." "I'm sure of that." Snake says as he sticks out his chest. Snake smiles as Ted chuckles.

"I have one more request I need you and your buddies to help me with but I'll call you with details later."

"Anything for you Mr. Ted." They shake hands. Ted leaves.

CHAPTER 14

On Thanksgiving Day Haddie's entire family, Sli, Snake, Diana, Bryk, Tyler, Tawny and Ted are all eating dinner and enjoying one another's company.

After dinner Ted remembers he left something in his car that he should've brought in. "Baby girl you feel like running down to my car and bring me the bag in the back seat?" He addresses Diana. "It's the brown paper bag.".

"Yeah." Diana nods. "Where yo' key at?" "Look in my coat pocket. Thanks."

Diana grabs her jacket, then Ted's car keys. Still wearing her slippers, she goes outside. Haddie brings out the photo album, despite the kid's and grandkid's grumbling against it.

She sits on the couch next to Ted, pointing at various younger pictures of each of her kids and grandkids while telling different stories about their lives.

Diana returns. "Is this the bag you wanted?" She lifts the contents out the bag. In one hand it looks like a disheveled wig. In the other hand there are dirty looking clothes. Everyone is looking puzzled at the items.

Ted jumps up from the couch, snatching the items from Diana, he shoves them back into the bag. "My nephew just leaves his stuff anywhere." Ted tries explaining. He reaches into the bag and pulls out a narrow gift box, the length of a watch. He sets it on the coffee table. "I'll take this garbage back on down to my car when I get ready to leave. Thanks baby girl." Diana hands him his car key. The room is awkwardly quiet.

Haddie lifts her eyebrows upon looking at the gift box but starts talking as if unphased. "The reason Snake and Sli got they nicknames is 'cause of the weird way they tried to crawl. Snake looked like he was slithering." Haddie wiggles her head and body while moving her arms as if she's crawling in place. "And Sli looked like she was belly surfing as she used her arms to move her entire body forward and backwards, sliding around. So Sli is short for slide." She says matter-of-factly then cracks up laughing. Everyone else either join in, chuckle or grin.

Immediately after back-down-memory-lane ends Bryk, Tyler, Tawny, Snake, Sli and Diana play video games. They talk Haddie and Ted into joining them in playing Super Mario 64 to get a good joke out of it. The kids show them what buttons to push to make certain things happen. When Ted and Haddie fail miserably the kids laugh hard and loud every time.

Even though Haddie and Ted makes it obvious they have no idea what they are doing they are determined to appear that they do. "Yall don't want none of dis!" Haddie yells while kicking her feet in the air and pushing all the buttons and ending her turn sooner than it could've been, had she known what she was doing.

"Oh yeah…You kicking they tails baby." Ted eggs her on as he turns his head away from Haddie and sticks out his tongue.

Moments prior to the football game beginning Rock comes in announcing, "I wasn't sure what time the game started but I'm not tryna miss not even the commercials, 'cause I got too much money ridin' on this one. So, we need to start celebrating my wins ret now!" He holds up a liter of Bacardi Gold Rum in one hand and a case of Miller Lite beer in the other.

Soon afterwards, Streng rushes in snatching off his coat and hat. "Maaan, dat game don't mean nothin' to me! Dey the ones gettin' millions to kill dey fool sefs. Only reason I'm watchin' 'em is 'cause I enjoy dem lookin' like dey 'bout to die." Streng laughs loud for a few seconds, then stops abruptly. "Ms. Haddie, can I get sumin to eat?" He grins excessively wide, then pulls his pants up only for them to slide down again.

Some time passes before the doorbell rings again. Snake answers it and Big Sheddy wobbles in scratching his head. "Hey yall. Mama Haddie, you mind if I fix me a plate 'fo the game start?"

The kids are still playing video games as the adults sit around chatting and listening to music. Streng and Big Sheddy are finally done eating, after three servings. They are slumped in their chairs at the dining room table, sipping alcohol from a red, plastic cup.

Ted gives Snake a secret nod. Snake starts the song "Ribbon in the Sky" by Stevie Wonder.

When the musical prelude begins, Ted acts shocked and pleasantly surprised that it's on. He jumps up from the couch and starts swaying and steppin' to the music. "Me and my boys won plenty of first place prizes at talent shows performing to this one here. Let me see…I would do something like a one two step." He moves around, as if trying to recall dance moves.

Diana looks at Ted awestruck. "Get outta here Ted! You don't even look like you could dance or sing." She cracks up laughing. Ted scrunches his face at her and continues dancing.

Streng jumps up from the couch to join Ted on his makeshift stage. "I'll be yo' back up dancer…Come on yall." Streng motions for Snake, Rock and Big Sheddy to join him. At first, they all appear to be uncoordinated and discombobulated. Ted begins singing:

> *Oh so long for this night I prayed*
> *That a star would guide you my way*
> *To share with me this special day*
> *Where a ribbon's in the sky for our love*

The backup dancers get in step with each other. Ted grabs Haddie's hand and kisses it as he continues singing.

> *If allowed may I touch your hand*
> *And if pleased may I once again*
> *So that you too will understand*
> *There's a ribbon in the sky for our love…*

The musical interlude begins. Ted and the dancers are coordinated in smooth dance moves, creating an uproar of excitement among their audience. Sli yells out, "Aw hell naw! Yall must've rehearsed this!" Haddie's blushing as she looks at Sli and nods in agreement.

Ted walks over to Haddie and pulls her gently to get her to stand. Haddie sways with him.

Ted continues singing in her ear:

> *This is not a coincidence*
> *And far more than a lucky chance*
> *But what is that was always meant*
> *Is our ribbon in the sky for our love, love*
>
> *We can't lose with God on our side*
> *We'll find strength in each tear we cry*
> *From now on it will be you and I*
> *And our ribbon in the sky Ribbon in the sky*
> *A ribbon in the sky for our love...*

When the musical interlude starts again, Ted gets down on one knee, as he opens the watch sized gift box, to show an engagement ring. Haddie is so stunned she backs up, dropping her ass right back onto the couch.

"Damn! That's a big ol' box for a ring." Sli yells.

Ted looks at Sli and smiles. "I was trying to throw your Mama off." He then looks at Haddie.

Tears trickle down her cheeks as she manages to muster a feeble and shaky, "Yes."

Ted gasps and drops his head. "Wait...What? You don't even know what you're saying yes to? I could be about to ask you to join me in a satanic cult."

Haddie moves her hands from her face and grins hard.

Ted couldn't help but to grin back. "Okay well that pre-answers the question I was deprived of asking."

Everyone bursts out laughing.

"My love, Haddie Maldive, thank you for agreeing to be my wife?"

All the females in the room are squealing. Streng, Rock and Big Sheddy stare emotionless.

Snake is grinning and recording them all.

Ted looks at the camera. "I guess this officially concludes my non-proposal." He shakes his head. Everyone cheers and applaud.

Diana is wiping tears from her face. Sli has her hands clasped together in front of her mouth, then releases them to say, "I knew yall were too coordinated for this to not be planned."

The teens go right back to playing their video game as they each yell out, Congratulations."

Tawny blurts out, "I was shocked to see Big Sheddy move like that." They all join her in laughter.

Everyone is congratulating and hugging Haddie and Ted. As the musical interlude continues playing, Ted is steppin' and beckons for Haddie to join him. They dance together until the song concludes, *"There's a ribbon in the sky for our looove."*

All is calm again before the football game begins.

****

On Christmas Day family members are in and out of Haddie's home, claiming they need to leave early due to other obligations. But Ted and Haddie are happy to spend a romantic evening together alone at Haddie's place. Or at least they try to with Diana still being somewhere in a nearby room.

****

On Sunday December 31, New Year's Eve Ted and Haddie enjoy an overnight stay atthe Carlton Ritz Hotel for Dinner, partying and drinking. They bring the new year in with lots of lovemaking.

"I love you, Haddie." "And I love you, Teddy."

CHAPTER 15

Haddie sits on the front porch, fanning herself with a small folded brown paper bag.

Ruby is walking deliberately slowly, while judgmentally staring at different things and people over the top of her glasses. She stops outside the wrought iron gate in front of Haddie's duplex, looking around to be sure no one is in earshot.

"Hey now, Haddie. I hear congratulations in order."

"Yeah chile." Haddie flashes her engagement ring. "Thank ya."

Ruby's face contorts into feigned excitement. "When Imma meet him?" "Maybe next time he over here."

"You got ya bride's gown already?"

"Not yet. I'll probably go sometime next week to look."

"I know Diana going with you." Ruby half asks and half declares.

"Chile you know she is. I can't fart without her telling me what it smells like." Ruby looks puzzled. "Oh yeah? How she do that?"

"Ma…you musta ate boiled eggs this morning? Or…that smells just like corn on the cob." Haddie says mimicking Diana's voice then goes back to her regular voice to explain. "'Cause you know that stuff don't ever digest. It comes right back out looking the same as it did when it went in."

"Well that's definitely a sho' sighn she crazy 'bout her Mama." Ruby reminds Haddie. "Yeah. Kids sho got strange ways of showing it don't they? She already said, Ma let's go looking for your dress after my dentist appointment next week." "Yall going to the bridal shop on Madison?"

"We might check some places out up there since that's where her dentist office is. So, I don't know yet. What's the latest, Ruby?" Haddie quickly changes the subject because it hit her that she'd better not discuss any more of her business with "running mouth Ruby."

Ruby perks up. "You know I got it for ya now don't ya. You heard Ms. Tinly's moving? Chile, she done let them grown ass kids of hers tear her shit up and now she foreclosing on her house."

"Aw naw." Haddie says empathetically, continuing to fan herself.

"The only way I knowed about it is the Sheriff's apparently didn't take time to stick the notice on her door properly 'cause it blew over on my front porch and stuck to my house shoes and that's when I looked down and saw it. Chile, I thought I had stepped on something' messy, like some gum or somethin'."

Haddie stops fanning. "Where she moving to?"

Ruby frowns up, tilts her head then bats her eyes. "Well now don't start me to lyin' but I hear she's lookin' into a nursing home." Ruby shakes her head and twists her face to appear sorrowful. "Lawd knows I hope I don't ever have to live or die in no nursing home."

"Hey li' ugly ass boy! Get out the street with that bike!" Tia yells, appearing out of nowhere.

Ruby jumps. "Don't be yelling in my damn ear!"

Tia scrunches her face at Ruby. "Whatchall talkin' 'bout?"

"Nothing!" Ruby blurts, then gets annoyed. "Whatchu want Tiawanna?"

Tia, holding the hair back from her eyes, rolls her eyes at Ruby. Tia breaks out into a happy dance—bopping, dipping, swiftly moving her feet and flailing her arms all while she's talking. "Ms. Haddie I'm so excited for you! Congratulations! Diana showed me the video of the proposal. It was beautiful. I want my boo to propose to me just like that, but instead of being on one knee he'll be doing a handstand."

Tia abruptly stops dancing then swiftly turns to point her finger in Ruby's face. "Now back to you."

Ruby knocks Tia's finger from her face. Tia keeps talking as if it didn't happen. "What I tell you 'bout calling me by my old government name? You know I gotta new government name now. And it's easy and simple. So, use it instead, Ms. Ruby! You wasting yo breath and poisoning my oxygen giving off so much unnecessary carbon monoxide using all these unnecessary letters, and long words and too many syllables. That's why the earth is so polluted as it is. Damn!"

Haddie tries to change the subject. "Ms. Ruby was just saying…"

Ruby blurts in. "Well, hell I just figured with all these different looks you should have a different name to match it."

Haddie tries again. "Ms. Ruby was just saying…"

Tia gets loud. "Aint no all these names! It's Tia." She claps her hand with each letter she spells. "T-i-a! That's it and that's all. I mean, Ms. Ruby, how hard could it be to remember three simple letters with only two syllables?"

"Ms. Ruby was just saying…" Haddie attempts yet again.

"As hard as it is to tell what you really is…You look like a man but yo' hair and body act like a woman. So, you a girl, boy, he, she, sissy swirl or what?" Ruby asks.

"What the fuck is a sissy swirl? You know what Ms. Ruby you need to go find yo' own business and stop minding other folks' stuff." Tia retorts, jerking her neck and snapping her fingers.

"Ha…like you got some." Ruby says. There's a few seconds of silence.

"Finally, as I was saying, Ms. Ruby was saying she didn't wanna end up in no nursing home like Ms. Tinly." Haddie interjects.

Tia looks stunned at Ruby then Haddie then back at Ruby. "What! Ms. Tinly aint in no nursing home. I just saw her go in the house not too long ago."

"Ms. Ruby say Ms. Tinly done foreclosed on her house and gots to go. The foreclosure notice got stuck to her shoe." Haddie tells Tia.

Tia jerks her head. "How a foreclosure notice get stuck to yo' shoe Ms. Ruby? They damn near be super gluing those papers to the door." Tia gets a look of revelation on her face. "Oooh…Is that what that paper said that was stuck on they door when you went over there to read it?"

Ruby looks stunned and embarrassed. "Now Tia who done started you to lyin'…" "Come on now Ms. Ruby. I seent you."

"You aint "*seent*" me do nothin' like that."

Tia tightens her lips. "Ms. Haddie, can I come up on yo' porch?"
"Yeah. Come on baby. The gate aint locked."

Tia reaches into her pocket and pulls out her flip phone as she walks up the stairs. She shows Haddie a video.

"Who dis is Ms. Haddie?" Haddie grins as she watches the video of Ruby looking around as she ascends a neighbor's steps, reads the notice stuck on the door, then looks around again as she goes back down.

Tia squeals with laughter. "I busted her ass. Caught straight on camera." Tia boasts and continues laughing loudly.

CHAPTER 16

Haddie has already tried on twenty-eight wedding gowns. Now on her twenty-ninth she poses, looking in the mirror. Diana sits watching, giving her opinions, flipping through a catalog of bridal party attire.

"Yo' weddin' is not gonna be nothin' like Rock's weddin'." Diana assures Haddie. "I mean that was crazy jacked up."

"No need to even compare anything of mine to any of yo' hood friends. A wedding reflects the bride and groom. So, ghetto is as ghetto does."

"That type of saying makes no sense to me, just like don't take no wooden nickels. Who da fu…" Haddie turns her head sharply in Diana's direction, slowly raising her eyebrows? Diana glances at her from the corner of her eyes. "Uuum…Wooden nickels don't even exist anyway."

Diana looks up from the magazine and stares when she notices Haddie is in a different dress. "Oh, that one is you, Ma." Diana walks over to look at the dress up close. "I thought you didn't want to wear white?"

"You must be color blind, gul. This is cream."

"Naw, Ma. I'm talking about something far from the white family… like orange or something. I think that would be the perfect color for you and it would still stand out from our peach dresses. Don't you think?"

Haddie turns toward Diana. Affectionately cuffing Diana's face in her hands, she looks her directly in the eyes. "Aaaw baby…I think that is such a lovely idea." Haddie smiles and nods before finishing her speech. "…for *your own* wedding!" Haddie turns back to face the mirror. "Hell naw! I aint wearing no damned orange. You tryna get me to look like the pumpkin at Cinderella's ball. Chile you done lost yo rabbit ass mind."

Diana goes back to sit down when a store rep walks over to them with a tray stacked with small clear plastic cups and a bottle of wine. "Would you ladies like some champaign?"

"No thank you. I need something on my stomach first. What time it is anyway?" Haddie asks.

Diana and the store rep respond nearly in unison. "Almost 1:30." The store rep is about to walk away.

Diana hesitantly puts up a finger. "Um…excuse me." The store rep turns around to look at Diana. "I'll take a cup of that." She pours the champaign and hands it to Diana.

Haddie turns her head to give Diana that oh really look then chuckles. "This should be interesting." She shakes her head.

Diana takes a sip. "Oh yuck. This is disgusting. How could a liquid be dryer than cotton balls? You got any juice or pop I can mix this with?"

"No, I'm sorry. Would you like me to throw it out?" Diana hands her the cup back and goes back to looking at the magazine.

Diana jumps from her seat with excitement. "Here it is! All the ladies should wear this dress but in peach!" She walks over to the full-length mirror where Haddie is standing.

Haddie looks at the dress, raises her eyebrows and twists her lip. "Uuummm. Nope!

That's only cute 'cause it looks painted on. Aint nobody gonna be able to breath in that." Haddie walks back into the fitting room.

"Aw come on, Ma! This would be the bomb on me."

"And only on you. The rest of them chicks are too meaty for that type of dress." Haddie yells.

Moments later Haddie exits the fitting room, dressed in her own clothes and carrying a cream-colored dress. She walks over to the store rep. "I'm gonna put this one on layaway." "No problem. Let me ring you up." Minutes later the rep gives Haddie a receipt.

Haddie turns toward Diana. "Let's go. I'm starving."

After they've finished eating lunch, Haddie and Diana stop by a bakery to check out wedding cake flavors and designs. Haddie takes note of three different ones she's considering. Diana snaps pictures of them.

When they're finally home and settled, they cozily sit on the couch, in their pajamas, re- watching the movie *Candy Man* and eating popcorn, while Diana is flipping through a magazine. "Oooo Ma! These chair covers in peach with some orange flowers as the centerpiece…um what they call those? You know like those cute ones with the dots on 'em that Auntie Zaney had on her dining room table that day we went over there?"

Haddie's forehead wrinkles, trying to remember. "I think you talking about lilies?"

Diana jumps with excitement. "Yeah! That's what Auntie Zaney called 'em. But those would be the only thing in orange though. Aw naw…wait a minute. We should do a bow on the back of the chairs, like these, in orange too." Diana points at an image. "The tablecloths should be peach, and the mats could be cream or the other way around."

"Chile you just determined to have orange somewhere. What is with you and this obsession with orange all of a sudden?"

"Ma now you know orange my favorite color but I'm just saying it's perfect with peach and cream. It makes everything really stand out. Look at this." Diana points at another picture.

Haddie stares at it in deep consideration. Diana continues. "With these cream-colored placemats aaand…okay the napkins should be orange too. With them folded in the center of the plates it would be popping! Just try to picture that, Ma. With the peach and cream in the background that brings out the splashes of orange everywhere else."

"I believe this time you do have a point with that orange stuff. I actually do like that.

Yeah, we can make that happen." Haddie says, nodding.

A huge grin spreads across Diana's face. She continues looking through the magazine while Haddie eats popcorn then grabs the remote to rewind the movie.

"Oooo! We can have the rehearsal dinner at that place Rock had his wedding reception.

That was a nice place."

"Yeah, The Chateau Bu'sche is beautiful." Haddie agrees.

"Okay I'll call to set that up because you know those places stay booked. Wait! Have yall even picked a date yet?"

"Next year sometime. I told Ted I want it in the Summer. I'm sure he's leaving it up to me to decide."

"Okay well pick it now so I can call." Diana presses. "Well since 711 is my favorite number…"

"Cool. July eleventh it is." Diana looks off into a daydream for a few seconds, then back at Haddie. "Well now that that's established, I already know where we're having your bridal shower." Diana gets a big grin on her face.

"Diana, you bet not be having no naked, sweaty strippers 'cause I'm too old for all that shit."

"Maaaa! Come on now you aint gotta get involved. Like you don't even have to touch his greasy, shiny buffed biceps, or that tight six pack, or even let him gyrate all over you so you won't have to feel everything through yo clothes, especially when he lifts you up in the air and make you bounce on his lap, or when he lay you flat on yo back and pump you so hard you can feel your tailbone kissing the floor." Diana stands up to demonstrate rough gyrating. "Not to mention the back of yo head scraping across the floor…with…each…thrust. And you gon' be praying yo' wig don't get caught on nothin'."

Haddie starts wiping her forehead and fanning her face with her hand. "Okay, okay. Just stop! Um…well…now that you put it all that way…Where we having my bridal shower?"

"I knew you'd see things my way." Diana says as she grins with pride. They burst out laughing.

CHAPTER 17

Snake is typing on the computer. The phone rings once when he snatches it up. "Snake's Auto. Hey, Brandon I was about to call you 'cause I was just looking over our inventory and apparently, only one of the parts for your car came in. So, I'm going to call them to find out what's the hold up." Snake scribbles on a pad:

Be sure to order other part for Brandon TODAY!

"Man, I apologize for the hold-up 'cause they usually on it at this company. But things like this tend to happen. Hopefully it'll be in no later than next week so we can get your car back running again as soon as possible…Man, thanks for under…"

Snake looks out his window to see a woman pointing a gun at Odeo. "Brandon we'll talk later. There's a situation I need to handle." Snake hangs up and kneels under his desk before dialing 911. "There's a woman with a gun…"

"Hold please." The emergency dispatcher interjects.

Snake gets the urge to pee since it felt like a long wait before the dispatcher finally returns. "What's your emergency?"

"There's a woman holding a gun to one of my employees. Send the police to Snake's Auto Repair, corner of Madison and California."

"What race is she?" "What?"

"Black, Caucasian, Hispanic, sir?" "Black."

"About how old does she look?" "I don't know."

"Twenties, thirties, forties, sir?"

Snake peeks out over his desk to get a look at the lady. "Thirties, I guess." "About how tall she is?"

"Look…" Snakesnaps.

"Listen sir an approximation is all I need. Just compare her to your height. Like isshe taller or shorter than you,sir?"

"I don't know! Lady look if I wanted to date her then that may be somethin' I'd care about but since she is about to commit a murder, fucking her is the last thing on my mind, so just hurry up and send the got damn police, now." Snake hangs up, peeks over his desk, stands, then timidly walks outside. "Could somebody tell me what's going on?"

Bells are jingling as Cooper is approaching on his bike.

> *Fresh off the freight, so you know it's great!*
> *My name is Cooper, but you can call me Coop.*
> *Accessories: from bangles, bags to boots.*
> *Got toys for yo' kids that can spin, sang, or shoot.*
> *Wanna eat?*
> *Got those sour, sugary, and salty treats.*
> *Need something at home?*
> *Check out my cutlery, candles, brushes and combs.*
> *If you need it, and I don't got it, just let it be known.*
> *I'll cop it when I can. I SWEAR the wait won't be long.*
> *Be back here in a flash; sangin' this same ole song.*

Everyone watches Cooper as he's passing by. The lady with the gun looks at Snake but keeps the gun pointed at Odeo. "This muthufuka told me my car was like new. I got as far as Pulaski and Madison when my shit cut off again. You think I was gonna walk back over here peacefully or without my piece? Fuck naw! Somebody gone go git my car, bring it back here and fix it for free."

"Beesh, jou don't even know what's wrong wit it. It could be sumding else..." Odeo says.

"Do I look like I give a flying fuck!" The lady cocks the gun and spreads her legs preparing for the kickback of pulling the trigger. "I gotcho beesh, mufuka!" "Okay...okay...Let's all just calm down." Snake says.

She grinds her teeth. "I *hate* that word *calm*, especially when I'm not!"

Snake slowly walks closer toward them. The lady swiftly aims the gun at Snake. "Don't come no closer." Snake stops.

Odeo raises his arms then drops them. "Maaan, dis is sum bullshit! Tankyzer, I fixed jour raggedy ass car…"

Snake looks puzzled at Odeo. "The fuck you just call her?"

Tankyzer aims the gun back at Odeo. "Oh, so now you gon' blame my car for yo' shitty work?"

"Odeo, don't say nothing else." Snake commands. "What? Oooh so now jour on her side?"

"This aint about sides. Remember your training? It's about excellent customer service." "Man fuck dat. dis beesh gotta gun on me. Proper customer handling is gone adios!" "Odeo! I need you to focus. This aint no time to be stroking your own fucking ego." "Aint dis sum shit. You supposed to be checking dis beesh not me."

"Aint nobody supposed to be checking me nothing. Call me one mo' beesh, mufucka! If you had done yo' job right in the first place you wouldn't be in this situation. Now let's go get to my car. Betta yet bring all yo' muthufukin' tools so you can fix it right where it is."

"Whoa…Okay…Wait a minute ma'am. First of all, he wouldn't know what tools to take, and it would be too heavy to haul them on a bus. Plus, it's not a wise idea for you to take him as a hostage. People go to jail for stuff like that." Snake tells her.

The lady starts flinging her arms around. Snake and Odeo duck. "All I know is somebody betta fix my mufuckin' car! NOW!"

Sirens are approaching. Several police cars pull onto the lot. An officer jumps out of his car with his gun drawn. "Drop the weapon now!"

Snake and Odeo run and duck behind cars. Tankyzer drops her head then her weapon makes a clunk sound as it hits the ground. "Now put your hands in the air and take five steps backward." She complies. An officer runs to her and puts handcuffs on her.

Rock walks out of the shop puzzled. "What the fuck is going on?"

Snake and Odeo stand up, staring at Rock, before walking toward him. "Man, where were you?" Snake asks.

"I was taking a shit." Rock says.

"Maaan, I take da rest of day off. I no 'preciate bein' t'rown to wolves 'specially the mad Black beeshy kind." Odeo says looking angrily at Snake and rolling his eyes.

CHAPTER 18

Haddie sits on the front porch fanning herself with a tattered notebook. Ruby is walking over deliberately slowly, while judgmentally staring at different things and people over the top of her glasses. She sees Tia is already standing in front of Haddie's gate. Ruby looks around to see who else is in earshot as she quietly stands beside Tia.

"Yall hear about all them break-ins around here lately?" Ruby asks.

Tia jerks her head in Ruby's direction. "Ruby! Where da fu…Ms. Ruby you almost made me cuss. Don't be sneaking up on me like that."

"Aint that nothing. You do it to me all thetime."

Haddie swats at bugs. "But you know I only heard about the house at the corner getting robbed. I didn't think much of it since they be having 24-hour company rotating in and out. I bet it's most likely somebody they be having in theirhouse"

"Oooh Haddie that's cute. Is that what they calling whore houses now? Twenty-four-hour company?" Ruby says.

"Uh uuuuuh." Tia blurts. They all burst out laughing.

"Ms. Haddie I'm surprised you aint barbecuing like you always do on the fourth of July." Tia says.

Ruby answers for Haddie. "I recon Haddie 'bout tired this year what with preparing for her wedding and all."

"Chile naw that aint it. You know I love cooking for a festive occasion. But er'body claim they gotta get up for work in the morning. And I aint doing all that work by myself."

"What job Diana gotta go to; Bedside Beauty, Incorporated?" Tia asks then laughs loudly and long. Ruby chuckles then stops abruptly when she sees Haddie's staring at her with a straight face.

"Oh, you got jokes, huh?" Haddie asks rhetorically. "You know darn well Diana enjoys being a kept woman, even if it is by her own mama…and brother…and sister who's doingit."

"Yall got that gul so spoiled. Her feet aint gon' hit the flo' til she forty." Ruby adds. "Ha! Not even then. More like damn near ninety." Tia states then laughs again,loudly and long.

"Yall better leave my baby alone!" Haddie says playfully.

Tawny walks up with three friends. "Granny can we play chess on yo porch?" "Yeah. Yall come on."

"Aaaaw. Aint yall cute in yall matching Independence Day costume colors." Tia announces.

Ruby stares up and down at Tawny and her friends. "Tawny you sho done growed up.

Yous a big gul. How old is you now?" "Seventeen." Tawney replies.

"Aint they just adorable." Haddie says with a big grin.

Friend one is staring at Tia. "Tia where you get that wig from?"

Tia looks Friend one up and down. "Yo mammy. You don't be asking me no dumb shit like that. You need to be tryna borrow her titties li' cardboard chested ass girl." Everybody bursts out laughing. Friend one rolls her eyes.

"Let me get on away from here 'fore I put a hurting on this li' heifa. I'll talk to yall later." Tia says as she walks away. Tawny and her friends go inside the building.

"Say…Ms. Ruby, since you're the first to hear about all the horrible things happening around here you could help make a change in the neighborhood. I attend the beat meetings every second Tuesday of the month at 6:30. You should come with me." Haddie says.

Tia and her friends return to the porch with a table and chairs, setting it up to play chess. Ruby frowns as if contemplating Haddie's request. She tilts her head then bats her eyes.

"Chile naw. Now don't start me to lying but I hear it aint nothing but a bunch of niggas rantin' about what's goin' on and it still aint nothin' changin' 'round here."

"Now *that* is a ball faced lie, Ruby. Didn't we get brighter lights on the block and a new traffic light at the intersection where the kids cross near the school?"

"Well yeah." Ruby nods in agreement. "So, you sayin' the beat meetings had something to do with that?"

"Whatchu thought that mayor Daley himself just took a stroll through our neighborhood and decided to get these problems fixed? This is why it takes a village. The more people involved the more likely we can improve our neighborhood." Haddie stands. With her back toward Ruby, she is fidgeting with her chair, when she whispers under her breath. "Always the complaining niggas aint gone do shit." Tawny and her friends giggle.

"What's that Haddie?" Ruby asks.

"Huh? Haddie faces Ruby. "Oh, I was just reminding myself the pilot on my stove needs to be lit…Well, Imma gone let yall have this porch. Time for me to start my dinner."

"Whatchu cooking?" Ruby asks. "Salmon, rice and fried green tomatoes."

"That sounds more like a down home breakfast than dinner, Haddie." "Yeah, well that's the best meal of the day anytime of the day."

"Maybe I'll fix myself some of that too. Good luck with that next beat meeting. Let me know how it turn out?" Ruby says as she begins walking away.

"You need to bring yo ass with me."

Ruby turns her head around and looks above the top of her glasses at Haddie, tightens her lips and walks deliberately slowly away, continuing to look around. Haddie goes inside.

Tawny and Friend one are playing a game of chess as Friends two and three are standing, and watching while eating bags of chips and discussing neighborhood drama. They get quiet when someone is about to make a play.

Tawny moves a piece. "Ha! Ha! Yall bitches bout ready to pay up." She leans back in her chair looking up and down the block.

Friend one focuses on the chess board a few seconds, before responding. "Talkin shit fo' it's even ova, huh? Don't end up gettin' yo feelins hurt again…withcho *banana head* ass."

"Wit a hunerd ridin' on dis here, I can talk all the shit I want… witcho UGLY ass!" Tawney blurts back.

****

Dusk is approaching. Tawny and her friend continue playing chess. Sli, Felanie, Big Sheddy and Streng are walking up the street heading toward the duplex apartment building.

Tawny's stretching when she looks up the block and spots them. "Aw shit here they come. Auntie Sli gon' be talkin' shit about whatever comes to her neck. Watch what I tell yall."

Sli, Felanie, and Streng walk up the stairs and stand on the porch. Big Sheddy remains at the bottom of the steps. Everyone acknowledges one another with either a nod or verbally.

"I see you got on some mo' new stomps huh Tawny." Sli says.

Tawny looks at each of her friends as if to say I told yall before responding. "Yeah bought these for a li' bit of nothin from Coop." Tawny holds her foot up to show it better.

"That dude know he be hustling on that bike though. I be seeing him er'where." Friend two says.

Felanie looks down at the shoe. "Aaaw…look atcho Rodomontade ass." Tawny and her friends look puzzled at one another and giggle.

"Exactly! Yall lookin like I spoke another language. Be sure to stay yall asses in school.

But for right now just go read a dictionary," Felanie instructs them.

Tawny rolls her eyes in her head. "In-tee-way…They hopped a freight train again. They say Coop's foot got stuck on the tracks just when a train was coming. Chopped all his toes off, but it obviously didn't stop him from riding that bike though." Tawny and her friends chuckle again.

"Dat nigga walkin around lookin' like Kunta Kinte now." Friend two hops in place on one leg while speaking with an African accent. "My name Toby now massa. Not Kunta Kinte no mo 'cause my *toe-be* gone." They chuckle and laugh, except Sli, who's shifting her eyes from each person in deep thought.

Friend three chimes in. "Yeah, now that mufuka give *free toes* a new meanin'." Friend three holds up a bag of Frito Lays corn chips. Big Sheddy shakes his head, chuckling along with the others who are laughing again, except Sli, who is now staring at Tawny.

"Maaan…Yall shawties ignant!" Big Sheddy says still shaking his head. "Yall can say whatchu wanna say. That aint stoppin' him from pushin' that bike and makin' his money though."

"Where you get the money from?" Sli asks more aggressively, as she towers over Tawny.

Tawny looks up at Sli.

"Damn auntie! Why you all up in my beeswax?! Do I ask you where you gitcho shit from? Can't you see I'm tryna win some Benjamins here? You fuckin' up my concentration and shit."

"Oh, so now you wanna show out in front of yo' li' nappy headed ass friends, huh?" "Wait…hold on," Friend three says. When Sli shoots an evil eye at her she looks quickly away, burying her head deeper into the bag of chips.

"Soon as you get through with this game come downstairs." Sli demands.

Tawny shakes her head, while looking at the chess board she responds, "I gotta make a run first…"

Slamming one hand on the table, while at the same time grabbing the back of Tawny's chair with her other hand, Sli bends over aggressively, which forces Tawny to look up at her. "Un un…whatever that shit is you talkin' 'bout can wait! As soon as this is ova, and be glad I didn't turn all this bullshit ova, bring yo black ass downstairs, and my table and chairs withchu."

"Yall know the real meaning behind the black and white chess?" Felanie asks. No one responds. Felanie scrunches her face and shakes her head. "See that's another reason yall dumb assess better stay in school. How could yall *not* see the obvious racism in the black and white chess pieces going against each other? Okay, you know what, I stand corrected 'cause you aint gon' learn nothing about that in nobody's school. But school could help you to interrogate things a bit profounder for yourselves. It's all up here." Felanie points to her head.

****

Sli, Felanie, Big Sheddy, and Streng watch as Tawny and Friends one and two walk into the basement carrying the card table and chairs, placing them in the corner where they originally were.

Sli looks at them with frustration then walks up to Tawny. "So Tawny...how'd chu get the stash fa them stomps?"

Tawny, Friends one and two look at each other. Sli glare at the friends. "Why da fuck is yall even still here?!" Sli yells as spit splatters in their faces. Their faces contort with disgust as they wipe it off.

Friends one and two walk out closing the door behind them. Sli nods. Big Sheddy grabs Tawny, as Felanie unwinds the duct tape and tears it with her teeth, while Streng rolls out plastic and repositions a chair on top of it.

CHAPTER 19

Bryk and Tyler are sitting on the living room couch playing a video game, intensely pushing the buttons on the controllers. Bryk slams his controller onto the couch, jumps up, picks it up again, tucks it under his arm and runs as if blocking players in a football game. "Ha Ha!

Toldchu I was gonna whoop yo ass son!" Bryk boasts. "Now pay up nigga!"

Tyler, still holding the controller, leans forward, placing his elbows on his knees. Looks at Bryk with raised eyebrows and calmly announces, "Maaan, I aint payin' you shit!"

Bryk dives on top of Tyler. They wrestle, knocking items from Haddie's coffee table. "The hell is yall doing in there?!" Haddie yells. Sitting on the toilet, she opens the bathroom door. "Yall bet not be in there breaking none of my shit!" They continue wrestling. Bryk hits the floor with a hard thud.

"Whatever the hell yall doing ya better stop fo I come out there, ass naked, and tear yall asses up!" Haddie yells before closing the door.

They are both panting. Tyler flops down on the couch, as Bryk climbs back on it. Tyler kicks the couch with the back of his heal. After struggling to stand up again, he looks angrily down at Bryk. Bryk scrunches his face as he looks up at Tyler. Bryk points at him and is about to say something, but then bursts out laughing.

Tyler stomps and jumps at Bryk pretending he's about to hit him. Before walking away, he kicks the side of Bryk's shoe. Bryk pushes Tyler. He stumbles into the table but stops himself from falling. "Granny you seent my bag?" Tyler yells.

Bryk grabs the game controller and begins playing a video game.

"Check the hallway closet. What's all in that heavy thang anyway! It's usually girls who overpack. You outdoing yo sister." Haddie yells.

Bryk bursts out laughing. "Aaaaaw ha ha haaaa…Granny say you pack like a girrrl," Bryk taunts, while rapidly and firmly pressing on the controller. "Granny whatchu tryna say he a faggot aint he!"

Tyler walks over to the couch, swings to smack Bryk on the head, but Bryk blocks it and ducks.

"Granny! Tell Tyler to stop hitting me!"

Tyler sneers at Bryk. "Now who the faggot? Snitch." Tyler walks to the closet to fetch his bag. He unzips it, looks inside, and grins. "I'm gone granny!" Tyler announces. "You gone where?" Haddie yells.

Tyler doesn't respond.

"Tyler! Boy I know you hear me!" Haddie yells louder. "Nigga you know you hear granny talking to you!" Brykyells.

The sensor beeps on the home alarm as the front door opens and shuts. Bryk shuts off the video game. "Granny Imma gone take the garbage out!"

"Make sure you tie that bag up tight and push that garbage bin lid all the way down 'cause those animals get in there when it's loose enough. At least, I guess that's who's doing it."

Bryk grabs the garbage bag and leaves out the back door.

Tyler is outside, at the bottom of the porch steps, when he realizes he doesn't have his cell phone. He drops the bag beside the steps and runs back up to Haddie's apartment. Again, the front door sensor beeps as it opens and closes.

Haddie is still in the bathroom. She yells out, "Bryk, you took the garbage out that fast?"

Tyler doesn't respond as he looks around for his cell phone. "Granny! You seent my phone?!"

Bryk drops the garbage bag into the trash bin in the alley and walks around to the front of the duplex. He sees a bag and looks inside. He smiles, zips it back up, slings it over his shoulder and walks away.

Tyler grabs his snapback cap, which is sitting on the dining room table, and puts it on his head. His Nextel phone was underneath it. He opens it to check the battery life, then snatches the phone charger from the wall.

"Naw…I aint *seent* yo phone. Booooi yall with these words. Where is you goin anyway!

Haddie yells. The sensor beeps again as the front door opens and shuts. The toilet flushes. Haddie washes her hands then walks out of the bathroom. "Anybody know where Tawny w…" Haddie looks around to see the house is empty. Her face frowns when she sees the what-knots are strewn about on the coffee table and along the floor. She picks up a Black, headless, ceramic figurine, then looks around for the head. She shakes her head. "Those damned boys."

Tyler returns to the side of the steps to grab his bag but sees it's gone. He looks around in panic. When he spots some people standing around, he runs to them asking if they've seen a bag. Some say no while others shake their heads. One person cusses him out.

As Tyler nears the end of the block, he spots Bryk some blocks away, standing at the bus stop, with the bag dangling from his shoulder.

Tyler runs full force toward him.

CHAPTER 20

Tawny is seated in a metal folding chair with both hands tied together behind her and each ankle tied to each leg of the chair. Coagulated blood is on her lips and above her eye. Her words are slurring as her chin rests on her chest. "Auntie...I don't know why you won't believe me. I didn't take yo stuff." Tawny speech is slurred.

Sli kneels into a frog position so that Tawny can look at her. "This is yo' second fucking time taking shit from me." Sli looks bewildered. "You here mostly all day and can tell me er' damn thang that goes on around here. So, if you don't have it then you should at least be able to tell me who does?"

Sli looks down at the concrete floor, shakes her head in disbelief, as she rises slowly. She glances at Big Sheddy, Felanie and Streng, then at the brick wall, squinting at a crumbling brick. "Damn! I wonder how that happened? I really need to get that fixed...Hey Big Sheddy!"

Big Sheddy jerks his head in Sli's direction. "I need you to make a run for me," Sli tells him, while looking angrily down at Tawny. "Okay...so actually you should be dead by now because this shit should not have happened to me twice by the same bitch. So, I'll let this slide one mo' again if you just give me my cash back, you can keep er'thang else."

Tawny begins crying. "But...I didn't take...yo stuff." She says between sobs "Well just tell me who did, and I'll untie you."

"I don't knoooow..."

"LIES!" Sli walks quickly into her bedroom, picks up a pillow and snatches the pillow case from it.

CHAPTER 21

The CTA bus slows down before coming to a complete stop where Bryk is waiting to get on. Tyler stops running toward it. He bends over to rest his hands on his knees, taking rapid breaths, with his head hung. A passerby asks, "Hey shawty? You need to go to the hospital or something?" Tyler is coughing and responds by shaking his head. He looks up, gazing at Bryk, who stands up from the bench to board the bus. People ahead of Bryk are slowly stepping onto the crowded bus.

"Bryyyk! Bryyyk! Bryyyk!" Tyler's yells with croakiness in his voice. "Muthafucka…I know yo ass hear me!" He takes a deep breath and blows it out slowly before trotting towards a run.

Bryk has on headphones and is fidgeting with his Walkman CD player while slowly inching up, waiting behind people for his turn to mount the bus.

Tyler runs frantically as he watches Bryk getting closer to boarding the bus. With only a few people ahead of Bryk, Tyler desperately looks around searching for a faster way to catch up to Bryk. "Bryyyyk!" Tyler notices a little girl riding a pink bike. She falls to the ground. He goes to her, picks up the bike and takes off on it. Someone chases Tyler to get the bike back, but he gets away.

Tyler, heading full speed toward the bus stop, rides on and off the sidewalks and streets. Drivers are blowing, pedestrians are yelling, some give him the finger. He is almost at the bus stop when Bryk steps onto the bus. Tyler is finally a few feet behind the bus when he jumps off the bike, stumbling, and leaving it in the street. He runs to the bus. People are walking down the stairs at the front and back. Tyler is pressing his way to get on at the front. "Bryk! Man, give me my bag! Bryk! Where you at, nigga? Hey Bryk! Hurry up and get yo ass off here!"

"Hey li' boy! Move ya ass and stop yelling in folks' ear! Show some respect and get out the way so they can get off!" The bus driver yells.

Tyler looks confused as he figures Bryk should've been stepping off the bus by now. He stops trying to mount the bus and waits for everyone to exit.

"Hey! Has anybody seen an ugly Black boy with a Black bag?" People continue stepping off the bus ignoring him. He steps back, checking to make sure Bryk didn't exit at the back of the bus. This is when he sees that directly in front of the bus he's standing near there is another bus pulling away. Figuring that must be the bus Bryk is on Tyler runs afterit.

"Heeeey! Stoooop! Wait! Somebody, stop that bus!"

Feeling defeated, Tyler walks slowly across the street to wait at the bus stop to head back home.

****

At Garfield Park people are barbecuing. Fireworks are popping, loud booms are setting off car alarms, and sparkles are lighting up in various areas. Bryk is among them. He has become the temporary ringleader of a group of children who are following his personal fireworks display. Bryk's bag is full of dangerous explosives—M-80s, M-100s, quarter sticks, half sticks, cherry bombs, and silver salutes.

A kid walks up to Bryk and asks if he could light his sparkle for him. Bryk points at the stick, bursts out laughing and pushes the kid's face away with the palm of his hand. The other children join in laughing. Bryk continues moving about the park lighting explosives.

Jingling bells are approaching before Cooper yellsout:

> *Fresh off the freight, so you know it's great!*
> *My name is Cooper, but you can call me Coop.*
> *Accessories: from bangles, bags to boots.*
> *Got toys for yo' kids that can spin, sang, or shoot.*
> *Wanna eat?*
> *Got those sour, sugary, and salty treats.*
> *Need something at home?*

Check out my cutlery, candles, brushes and combs.
If you need it, and I don't got it, just let it be known.
I'll cop it when I can. I SWEAR the wait won't be long.
Be back here in a flash; sangin' this same ole song.

A man, wearing dark sunglasses and a baseball cap, is intently watching and following Bryk.

CHAPTER 22

Sli shoves the pillowcase into Big Sheddy's chest. Big Sheddy grabs ahold of it. "Go fill this up with at least six loose bricks...from *outside*." Sli points at Big Sheddy but speaks toward Streng and Felanie. "I have to stress outside 'cause this slow nigga would get to pullin' the loose bricks off the walls in here and shit." Sli turns to Big Sheddy. "Now how many bricks do I want?"

"Six." Big Sheddy replies with a nod.

Sli speaks slowly "No...more. No...less.".

"A'ight boss." Big Sheddy salutes then wobbles toward the door. When he opens it, Tyler has his hand in the air about to knock.

"What's up Shawty?" Big Sheddy asks playfully, looking down on Tyler.

Everyone looks toward the door to see who Big Sheddy is addressing. Tyler tries going around and even pushing him. When he doesn't budge, Tyler gets irritated. "Maaaan...Move yo big ass out my way!"

"Go findchu some bidness, shawty?"

Tyler continues pushing. "I'm looking for my Sista, nigga. Now move!" Tyler tries tackling Big Sheddy only to bounce off his stomach and into the wall behind him.

Big Sheddy chuckles. "You must got a death with...fool." "Go find you somewhere to play, Tyler!" Sli yells out.

"Auntie! I'm looking for Tawny!" Tyler says still scuffling to move Big Sheddy.

Sli rushes over to the door, shoving Big Sheddy and Tyler out, closing the door behind her. "Gone 'head take care of that," Sli says addressing Big Sheddy. "I got this."

Sli grabs Tyler's shirt collar then slams him against the wall. "Listen here you li' punk! A lot of my shit is gone! Where is it?"

"Let me goooo!" Tyler says as he squirms trying to break free of Sli's grip. Sli slaps him. "Answer me! You got my Shit?"

"Naaaw! Let me go!"

Haddie hears the commotion and opens the door to her apartment. "What's going on down there? Tyler that's you?"

Sli raises her eyebrows and widens her eyes as she gazes into Tyler's eyes. "He's fine, mama. Just down here playin' around again. Aint that right, Ty?" Sli squints her eyes and puts her face closer to his.

"Yeah…Granny I'm good."

"Sli, I need to wash. Did you finally finish washing your clothes?"
"Yeah, Ma."

"Okay. When Diana gets back, I'm gonna send her down with a load. You gonna be there to let her in the laundry room, or should I give her the key?"

"I'll be here." Sli responds, still glaring at Tyler.

As Sli mildly loosens her grip on Tyler's shirt, he snatches away. Tyler is walking sideways slowly upstairs, toward Haddie's apartment, angrily looking down at Sli. He pretends to scratch his head with his middle finger directed at her. "Granny you seen Tawny?" Tyler asks.

Sli points angrily at him, semi-whispering between clenched teeth, "You bet not be lying to me or it's yo ass." Sli warns him before going back into her apartment.

Sli is pouring herself a glass of whiskey, when Felanie exits the bathroom, wobbling, mocking Big Sheddy. She plops down on the couch. "Maaaan it's axiomatic dat mufuka sho needs to lose at least two hunerd pounds fo his big ass die from just walkin'. I betcha if he ends up in da penitentiary that weight'll drop off. Won't be no mo all you can eat buffets of greasy meats, biscuits, beans, bacon and buttered burritos for his esurient ass. We'll be calling *his* ass the Reverend Al Sharpton." Felanie laughs loudly at her own joke. Streng grins as he joins Felanie on the couch.

After Sli gulps down her third glass of whiskey, she throws the glass against the wall directly above the couch where Felanie and Streng are seated. They duck as glass shatters above them. "Damn girl! Yo fuckin' answer to er' god damn thang is da fuckin' penitentiary!" Sli yells.

Felanie and Streng look up at Sli in shock. "Wha da fuuu!" Streng yells.

****

Haddie is cooking dinner while Tyler is playing a video game. She steps into the doorway where Tyler is, staring at him as she wipes her hands on a dish towel.

"Where were you earlier? And where's Bryk and Tawny? You know better than to leave here without telling me where you going. I know you heard me asking you before you left out.

"Yeeessss granneee."

"Yes granny what? You still aint answered my question." "I was going outside."

"I know that knucklehead. Outside where?"

"Just outside, granny. Nowhere. I don't know where Tawny and Bryk at. I saw him get on the bus earlier."

"On the bu...? Does Sli know?"

Tyler grunts and humps his shoulders. "That's what I was trying to find out 'cause I was asking for Tawny, when I was down there, but she started hollerin' at me, so I just walked away."

"Let me call downstairs to let Sli know what's going on," Haddie says as she turns away from Tyler. "He knows betta than to be leaving from around here..." She continues fussing.

Tyler suddenly gets a thought, slamming the controller onto the couch. "Granny, I think I know where Bryk went! I'm going to get him!"

Haddie peeks from the kitchen to ask, "Whatchu talkin' 'bout?" Tyler is opening the door to leave. "I bet he at Garfield Park."

"Why would he be there?

"Uuum..." Scratching his head, Tyler's eyes dart around searching for a believable response. "Most likely watching fireworks...but Imma go see." Tyler runs downstairs then runs right back up. "Granny can I get some bus fare?" Tyler asks out of breath.

Haddie is stirring the contents in the pot. "Aw naw! You aint got no business on no bus this time a night."

"Please Granny! I'm seventeen years old now. I'll be legally a man next year. I can take care of myself. I promise." He grins and tilts his head.

"Boy…You aint nothin' but a charmer. Just like yo daddy. Go look in my change purse." Tyler kisses Haddie on the check then runs to her room, gets the money and runs back out the door.

"You betta be careful out there!" Haddie yells as she continues preparing dinner. The door sensor beeps as Tyler opens and closes it.

CHAPTER 23

Bryk's bag of explosives is getting low. His entourage has returned to their family's areas of gatherings. Bryk takes a break alone, sitting near a tree drinking a coke.

The man in the dark sunglasses leans against the tree beside Bryk. "Yo shawty! What's jour name?" The man asks.

Bryk looks up at him, then takes a swig of his Coke. "Nonya."

"Nonya? What type o'name is that for a li' boy, eh? You Hindu or sumting?" The man stares into Bryk's face. "Wait…Aintchu Snake boy?"

"Nonya damn bidnis is what I'm really sayin'! Maaan who is you and da fuck you askin' me all these questions fo?" Bryk gulps down the last sip of his drink, jumps up and quickly walks off, carrying the empty can to his next destination.

CHAPTER 24

Felanie cuts her eyes at Sli, stands up, walks slowly up to her with fists clenched and teeth grinding. "Yeeeeah...Well I should know...since I spent my time in there fa yo ungrateful ass. But let's just see if *that* shit *ever* happens again...So my advice is don't fuck nothin' else up... *next* time."

Sli balls up her fists. With her jaw muscles clenching and nostrils flaring, she steps closer to Felanie. "Let's just say that right about now is when you get tired of throwin' that bullshit back in my face. Oh, and I don't take kindly to threats 'cause it could easily be *you* sittin' in dat foldin' chair...Ya feel me?"

Their stare down gets too uncomfortable for Streng as he looks back and forth at them, holding his breath, wondering what to do. Streng didn't catch what their conversation was about, but he knows not to ask questions. He sees that both of their lips have stopped moving and figures it's safe to speak.

"Yall think the Bulls gon' win a fifth championship next year?" Streng asks hesitantly.

Sli and Felanie slowly stand down. Felanie, walks toward the couch, throws both hands in the air before slamming herself down onto the couch again. "Maaaan don't bring that Buuull shit up. I'm still cleaning up these lunk head ass niggas mess. They dumb assess don't know how to have a courteous celebration and act civilized. Oooh nooo. They gotta tear shit up looting and carrying on. I was one of those 650 people arrested they were reporting on the news. I was just cruising through checking out the scene when Five-O got up behind me and pulled me over to give me a DUI. And I didn't even have that much to drink. So now my community service punishment is cleaning up yall mess." Felanie looks wide eyed at Streng. "'Cause, Streng, I know yo' metal head ass was out there." She pushes Streng's head so hard his whole body falls over onto the couch.

"Hey! Da fuuu…But I betcha I got me a brand new tv though and some new stomps." Streng says, sitting up and lifting his leg to show his new Air Jordan gym shoes. "Fwee…and I got me some new Nike sweat suits. Fwee. And snap backs too. Fwee."

Felanie shakes her head. "And about what you were speaking on earlier, hell yeah, they gon' win again. Pockets are being greased 'cause agreements are being made under the table. I keep tryna tell yall those damn games are all fixed. Gon' make me belligerent all ova again."

Streng leans forward yelling out in laughter. "Aw now der you go wit dat conspiwacy bullshit."

Felanie waves both her hands dismissively. "Think about that shit. They already know Michael Jordan can play a whole team by himself and win. That's been proven when Scottie and Dennis didn't show up that time and Michael had no one backing him up."

Streng slaps his forehead. "Is you cwazy! Michael got lucky dat time but if it wasn't fa Pippen and Wodman he wouldna made it this faw. Don'tchu wememba Wodman was fuckin' niggas up when he was wit' Detroit. If he didn't bwing dat wild ball playin' to da bulls dey wouldn't be shit."

"Now I'll give you that." Felanie agrees. "And po' Pippen is getting' no proper justification. They're paying him the least among the three and he's like Mike's right hand man. But Rodman is a troublemaker and causing all kinds of distractions with all that ghetto ass ball playing that you sucking his ass about." Felanie shows a grin so hard her lips look distorted. "Look atchu takin' up for yo flamin' ass, faggoty ass boy…Dennis Wo-o-odman." Falanie says mocking Streng. She then flicks her wrists twice so that her fingertips lightly taps Streng's knee. "If he gets more enthralled about the game than he is about havin' bright ass rainbow ass hair fashion shows they gon' definitely take all the championships from here on out, as long as none of them gets traded."

"You damn stwaight they will. Maaan, you don't get it. Wodman is cool as hell. People just don't understand him. People wearing out that tired song 'Like Mike, if I could be like Mike.' Dennis Wodman should've been picked as the real MVP. And you know damn well dat man aint gay, Felanie. Er'time the camera on him he got him a white woman. Dat's a badass bwuda dere."

"Yeeesss, heee sssure isss." Felanie says as she jumps up from the couch, switching harder than necessary as she walks. Flicking her wrists and rapidly blinking her eyes, she puts her hands on her waist, spinning excessively to change directions, walking back and forth. She stops abruptly, feigning an overly feminine basketball dribble and toss. When she sits back down, Streng falls off the couch laughing loudly.

Felanie bends down to shout in his face. "That's right boo! Keep pubbing yo' man." Streng abruptly stops laughing and looks at Felanie with evil eyes.

CHAPTER 25

Bryk gets a cynical grin when he spots geese floating in the pond. He punctures a hole in the empty can, puts an explosive in it, then sets it close to the pond's edge.

The man in the dark sunglasses walks up close behind Bryk, almost whispering in his ear. "Li' man I wouldn't do dat if I was jou." He says between sucking his teeth.

Bryk, startled, turns around quickly and backs away. "Why the fuck is you following me dude? What are you some sort of faggoty ass child molester?"

The man lets out a loud diabolical laugh. Then looks at his fingernails, continuing to suck his teeth. "Jou know...dat watch looks reeeal expensive. And dat fancy chain 'round jour neck, wit dat heavy ass emblem dangling from it...I always wanted jewelry jus' like those."

Bryk looks down at himself. Quickly places the chain under his shirt. Then puts both hands behind his back.

The man shrieks with laughter again. "Jou know vat else...all those fireworks can't be jours, either. So, I'm sure jour already in troubul."

CHAPTER 26

The basement door flies open. All eyes shift to Big Sheddy as he wobbles in and drops the bag full of bricks next to Sli, who is sitting at the table. Big Sheddy is breathing heavily. "Maaan…I had to walk all the way up to Jackson and Sacramento to get dese from dat vacant lot. Yall know where they tore down Gray's liquor sto', across from that hotel. Found me a $20 bill too." He holds up the money with both hands, snapping it open.

Sli snatches it. "Like I give a fuck." She pockets the money.

Felanie crinkles her face, staring at Big Sheddy. "Damn dude. Why're you looking like it poured down raining on your ass? I'm gonna plant a $20 bill up there er'day. Get you to steppin'…" Felanie stands up to march in place. "Drop that weight yo ass just might live longer." "Maaan. Fuck you! You'll die befo' me. Yo big ass the one needs to be steppin'! I'm bout gettin' tired of yo bitch ass for real."

Laughing, Felanie claps her hands. Then abruptly stops. "That's probably about the most intellectual words you've said since yo immense ass last sucked yo mama's tit aint it?"

Sli slowly walks over toward Tawny wrapping the open end of the pillowcase around her hand.

Felanie jumps up from the couch. "Yo! Sli…let me holla atcha ova here for a sec."

Sli jerks her head toward Felanie with bucked eyes. "Bitch…This betta be worth it." Sli drops the bag beside Tawny and walks over to Felanie.

Felanie whispers, "Look lady. Contemplate on what you're doing right now."

Sli waves her hands and jerks her neck. "Wouldcho drop out ass stop tryna talk all educated and shit!"

"Okay, Okay. This is your only niece. I'm sure after all the pain you've already put her through, she woulda talked by now if she actually had yo' shit."

"Naw! Fuck That! That was the mistake I made the first time I let her get away with this bullshit. This shit don't get to happen a third time."

Sli walks back over to Tawny. "As much as I love you, niece I really hate you had to go there with me. But I need to show you and er'body else who tries to fuck over me that disrespect is not an option." Sli slowly looks at everyone in the room to make sure they heard and understood her. She twirls the pillowcase. "At least not in this lifetime."

CHAPTER 27

An angered Bryk walks up on the man, looking up into his face. "Maaaan I don't know who the fuck you is but I'm bout sick of you tryna get all up in my bidnis!"

"Jou betta get the fuck out my face 'fo I put a hurtin' on ya son." Despite the man's tone his expression remains calm. He snatches a gun from his waist but holds it close to his own stomach so no one else could see it. Bryk steps back frightened.

"Oooh…jou scared of this?" The man asks sarcastically. He shakes the gun in his hand. "I'm not gonna kill ya li' dude. Now…Let's just make a deal. I already know jou Snake's family. So, jou just hand over all dat gud shit jou stole from whoever, keep playin' witcho toys and dis…" The man extends his arm, moving the gun in a circular direction around Bryk. "…will all be our little secret…No?"

Bryk thinks about it for a few seconds. "I don't know what da fuck you talkin' 'bout!" He walks back toward the explosive in the can, near the edge of the pond, lights the stem and runs away.

After waiting a few seconds, the fire fizzles out. Bryk walks back to the can to relight it. It explodes. Fire attaches to the hem of Bryk's loose shorts, rapidly spreading onto the lower half of his body and onto his bag. The rest of the explosive's in Bryk's bag continue blowing up, one after the other. People watch in horror.

The man snatches off his sunglasses and baseball cap. Once the explosives stop, he rushes to kneel beside Bryk, lightly swatting at flames, and quickly removing Bryk's necklace and watch. Snatching the bag from under Bryk, he searches frantically through the pockets. He finds a wad of money wrapped in a rubberband and shoves it down the front of his underwear. He winces as the paper cuts his dick and pulls his pubic hairs. He then stands up, looking around. "Help! Somebody call 9-1-1!" He yells as he backs slowly away from Bryk and blends in with the gathering crowd. His mouth forms a crooked smile to reveal his glistening goldtooth.

****

In another area of the park, Tyler hears fireworks popping incessantly. A child is running toward his family. "Mommy! Some boy on fire over there!"

Hearing this Tyler runs in the direction where the kid pointed. The sound and sight of sirens and flashing lights are approaching.

Tyler presses his way through the crowd and sees it's Bryk. He drops down on his knees and lies on top of him. He yanks on him. "Bryk. Bryk…wake up. Say something, man. Bryk!

Noooo! Bryk, get up! Bryyyk! Get uuup!" Tyler cries as he buries his face in Bryk's chest.

Paramedic one tries yanking Tyler away from Bryk. "Let me go! This my cousin!" Tyler musters between sobs.

"What's your cousin's name?" "Bryk."

"That's his government name or nickname?" "I don't know. What you mean?"

"Don't worry about it. What's his last name?" "Maldive" Tyler continues sobbing.

"Maldive like the island?" "What?"

"Okay…you know what…if you wanna help your cousin you need to get up and out the way so we can take care of him. Where are his parents or your parents?" Tyler stands up but continues looking down a Bryk, sobbing, as the paramedic two begins working on Bryk.

"At home…I guess," Tyler answers.

"Is this your cousin's bag?" Paramedic one asks, while holding it up. Tyler nods in response. Having forgotten all about the bag, he looks terrified as she goes through each pocket. Finding nothing she gives the bag to Tyler.

"We need to get him to the hospital ASAP!" The paramedic two interjects. Both paramedics lift Bryk onto the gurney, then into the ambulance.

"Are there any adults related to you in the park?" Paramedic one asks. "No. Can I go with you?" Tyler asks.

"I'm sorry there needs to be an adult with him. I'm gonna need you to find his parents and tell them we're taking him to Cook County Hospital. You got that?" Tyler nods.

Sirens are sounding and lights are flashing as they run through red lights. Paramedic two begins administering CPR on Bryk.

****

When they arrive at Cook County Hospital both paramedics are running alongside Bryk as they push him on a gurney into a room in the emergency department. They transfer Bryk onto a hospital bed. A doctor is yelling orders as nurses and doctors are scrambling to give Bryk the needed medical attention.

Paramedic two is barking out stats and giving details. "We have a minor named Bryce Maldy. At least I think that's what his cousin said his name is. Anyway, his heart stopped on our way in. I administered CPR to stabilize him. His blood pressure was..."

"There's barely a pulse now! His blood pressure is dropping fast!" A doctor interrupts. "His heart stopped! Defibrillator!"

The defibrillator whirs. The nurse places the gel on the pad, rubs them together, and yells, "ALLCLEAR!"

CHAPTER 28

The brick filled pillowcase pounds into Tawny's chest. Sli drops them to the floor.

Tawny, gasping to breath, coughs uncontrollably. A loud thump is heard above the basement apartment. Everyone looks at each other.

There's the sound of someone running on the stairs. The basement door flies open. It's Diana. Diana is breathing heavily, stares with her mouth open. "What's going on here? Is that Tawny?"

Sli walks up on Diana, preventing her from stepping into the apartment, and blocking her view. "Why you didn't knock? Whatchu want?" Sli says.

"Water...I just need water." Tawny says, barely audible.

"I can't believe you're doing this." Diana says, shaking her. Her look of disbelief slowly changes to disgust. "You're right I shouldn't be down here. What the fuck you care that your Mama just passed out on the kitchen floor 'cause she got a call that her grandson, *your only son Bryk*, was just rushed to the hospital."

Sli looks stunned, then begins semi-hyperventilating. "What happened?"

"I don't know. Somebody just called Mama and said he was at Garfield Park when the ambulance took him to Cook County Hospital. Next thing I know Mama fell out the chair."

Sli manages to transform herself back into calmness, while silently seething, before speaking. "Okay. Let me finish taking care of this and I'll be heading over there." Sli puts her hand on Diana's shoulder and gently pushes her backward, before closing and locking the door.

Diana is about to run upstairs but instead she kicks the door several times with the bottom of her foot, then turns around to continue ranting. "Yeah...Mama's okay. I got her up off the floor so she can get dressed so *we* can go to the hospital and check on *yo'* child! Ya evil ass whanch!" She runs upstairs.

Sli is in deep thought and slowly pacing the floor. Moments later footsteps are heard coming back down the steps. The outside door of the apartment building squeaks as it opens. Sli rushes to the door to look out. "Call me when yall find out what's going on." Sli says as she steps out to hold the outside door open for Haddie and Diana. "I'll be there soon."

"You need to be coming with us to see about your son." Haddie says. Diana is assisting Haddie by the arm as they descend the outside stairs. With their backs to Sli, Diana sticks up her middle finger.

Sli slams the door and returns to the basement. "Now...Where was I? ...Oh yeah..." She grabs the pillowcase filled with bricks, swings it a few times then whacks Tawny across her head and again on her neck. Tawny's body, and the chair, slams down hard onto the concrete floor.

Blood oozes slowly across the, from under her head. Felanie, Streng and Big Sheddy walk over to look.

"Damn girl! I didn't think you were takin' it this far!" Felanie panics. Streng looks into each of their faces before asking, "Is she still breathing?" "Now what the fuck we..." Big Sheddy wanted to ask.

Sli cuts him off. "Don't go to asking dumb ass questions, man. It's business as usual." "Come on now, Sli! We aint never had to do no shit like this to fam..." Felanie says. "Fuck family! Yall know I don't like repeating myself. Now get it done!" Sli commands.

CHAPTER 29

The waiting room of the Cook County Hospital's emergency department is jammed with Maldive family members, relatives and friends. A nurse comes out, excusing herself, as she wheedles her way through the crowd, stopping in the middle of the waiting room. "Which one of you is Bruno Townsmend?" She asks.

"He's over here." A man, standing near Bruno, points to him.

The nurse walks over to Bruno, who is wearing a do-rag. A dingy white wife beater t- shirt peeks between the zipper area of a thin blue windbreaker. Both sleeves are pushed up to his elbow, but only one pant leg on his blue jeans, which is stained with sporadic dirt patches, is rolled up to his knee.

Someone gets up from their seat next to Bruno to allow the nurse to sit down. "Hi Mr.

Townsmend. I'm Nurse Jersie. I need to ask you some questions. Is that okay?"

Bruno nods his head. "Yeah. Sure." "How are you related to the patient?"

"I'm the dad. You know what I'm sayin'." Nurse Jersie writes on the form. "Okay. Is it a male or female?"

"Male. You know. It's my son. Know what I'm mean?" Nurse Jersie nods and writes again.

Okay. We've had quite an influx of traumas tonight. So, I'm going to need you to complete these forms." Bruno takes them. Nurse Jersie stands. "When you're done, just bring them back up to the desk, along with valid ID."

Bruno nods while patting himself, as if searching for ID. "Thank you." Nurse Jersie says before walking away.

Once Nurse Jersie is out of sight, Bruno turns to whisper to the man next to him. "Yo cuz, you got yo' ID withchu? I left mine athome."

"Stop lyin' nigga. You know damn well yo' license got revoked." Bruno's cousin says as he takes his ID out his Pocket and hands it tohim.

"Thanks, cuz. You gone be his daddy for now…cool?"

"Maaan… Gone somewhere with that." The cousin says as he adjusts himself in his seat.

Glancing over the forms Bruno's face scrunches. He looks up in frustration, throwing his hands up. "Why Sli not here?"

A lady, across the room, notices Bruno struggling and walks over to help him complete the medical forms. "I sho appreciate yo' help auntie," Bruno says, handing her the clipboard.

Once the forms are complete, Bruno walks to the desk, handing the forms and his cousin's ID over to the receptionist. The rep makes a copy of the ID and gives it back to Bruno who returns to his seat.

Time passes. Bruno returns to the nurse's desk. "I've been waiting over half an hour! You know what I'm sayin'? Come on now! I need to see my son! What's going on? Why was he even brought here?"

"I'm so sorry for the wait, Mr. Townsmend. Our director of nursing felt we needed to contact the police…"

"The police! Wait! What are you tryna to say? What we need them for!" Bruno says with a hint of fear and anger in his voice.

The phone rings. Nurse Jersie excuses herself. Bruno waits impatiently until she hangs up. "Okay Mr. Townsmend." She picks up the clipboard that Bruno turned in. "You stated that Bryk is age fourteen, approximately five feet, 140 pounds. So, here's the problem: There are several young men who were brought in here this morning, closely fitting this description."

Bruno's eyes shift as if searching for an answer. "Well then since all the patients are unconscious just let me go back there and check for myself. I've watched my own son sleep all his life. I'll recog…"

"I'm so sorry Mr. Townsmend." Nurse Jersie cuts in. "I know how frustrating this is for you, but we cannot let you in the patients' rooms due to confidentiality purposes. As soon as an officer arrives, I will bring him to you."

Bruno hesitates before responding. "A'ight," He finally says, sounding defeated, before somberly walking away, dragging his feet, with his heels smashing down the back of his six- month-old Air Jordans.

CHAPTER 30

Big Sheddy, Streng and Felanie are nailing eight-foot-long, two by four wooden boards together; layered on top of each other, like how Popsicle sticks are glued together to make a miniature house, but in this case the boards are being stacked together to form a casket. They even cut smaller pieces to insert into the head and foot areas of the casket, once the body is inside, to enclose the open ends.

As they are finishing up a car slowly cruises through the alley. The driver stops, lowering his tinted window just enough to show his forehead. "Yo...Where Snake be at?" A man's voice asks.

"Wrong address!" Big Sheddyreplies.

The driver laughs maniacally. "Okay well if he happens to come back home jou be sure to tell him I owed him one, so he'swelcome."

Big Sheddy, Streng and Felanie look at one another. "Who the fuck is you?" Felanie asks.

The driver laughs again and drives away.

As they continue working, the curtain in the nosy neighbor's window swings lightly as it falls back into its hanging position.

Big Sheddy, Streng and Felanie carry the makeshift casket into the basement apartment and set it on the floor. Big Sheddy and Felanie wrap plastic around Tawny's body then lie it inside the casket. Streng cleans up the blood on the floor. Felanie goes out to the front of the house where the pickup truck is and brings it to the back. They carry the casket to the truck, then stack the remaining loose two-by-fours on top of the casket and strap it all down.

Felanie gets behind the steering wheel, Sli sits in the passenger seat, Big Sheddy and Streng are in the backseats.

CHAPTER 31

An officer finally arrives at the hospital. He escorts Bruno, Haddie and Diana into a private room. The officer looks at a paper, waiting for everyone to get seated. The voices, chiming in and out of his radio are barely audible as everyone pulls a chair from the huge wooden conference table to sit down.

Bruno, Haddie and Diana sit silently staring at the officer, then looking puzzled at one another, which seemed like way too long, before he finally looks up from his paper to address them. "Okay so I've been called here for a couple of reasons. One is because, according to the ambulance report, a minor was alone, and without adult supervision at the park, when he was injured. The second is, we need to identify and unite you with the correct person. One way we could go about identifying him, which is one I'm not fond of, is if your son has a criminal record, we could check fingerpr…"

"Naw man, my son aint no criminal. You know what I'm sayin'?" Bruno interjects. "Okay well that eliminates that option. According to the report and based on what you all are saying there's a strong possibility that it was most likely your son who was brought in." The officer looks at the paper in his hand. "They also have here what looks like the naaame…" The officer squints to make out the writing. "Bruce Moldy? But you're saying your son's name is Bryk correct?" They nod and say yes in agreement.

"Yeah, um, it's spelled…" Bruno twists his lip while looking at the ceiling. "Um, B-R- ah-Y-K," Bruno says, grinning.

The officer raises his eyebrows as he writes on the paper. "Wow! They really botched this up. Well, I guess that's what this is supposed to read. Could you spell the last name forme?"

"M-a-l-d-i-v-e," Diana spells quickly, looking at Bruno with irritation.

"Thanks," The officer says, then looks up to address them. "But with noID....Well anyway since all of the unidentifiable patients have a bag of clothes in their rooms if you could tell us what Bryk had on…?"

Bruno turns to look at Haddie. "He was staying with his granny this week." He rubs the side of his nose, using a rapid circular motion with the palm of his hand. The sound of loose snot reverberates throughout the room. Diana's face contorts in disgust as she stares at Bruno.

Haddie's shaking her head, staring at the table in deep thought. "I was in the bathroom when he said he was gonna take the garbage out. He was supposed to come right back in but never did."

Diana, shaking her head says, "I wasn't home."

"Is there anything else any of you can think of that you wanna tell me that may help distinguish Bryk from the rest, like a tattoo, scar, skin tags, birthmarks, anything?" The officer asks. Everyone shakes their head.

"Naw. Well, now I don't know if this would help but my other grandson, Tyler, did say he thought Bryk would be at Garfield Park. So, it's a possibility that Bryk was brought here. I gave Tyler bus fare so he could get on the bus because he begged me to let him go look for Bryk. I've been trying to call both of 'em, but I haven't heard back from nam one of 'em," Haddie says, placing both hands on her head. "Lord have mercy. I hope theyokay."

"Well, Officer, could you at least tell me why he was brought here though…You know what I'm sayin'?" Bruno asks.

"I'm gonna send a doctor in to speak to you about that. Any of you have a picture of him on you? I may still be able to recognize him even if he's sleeping."

Haddie fishes around in her purse and pulls out a wallet sized photo. "This is one he took at school, two years ago, but his looks ain't changed much since. At least I don't think so. "

Haddie's eyes water. "Oh Lord my baby back there all alone. Probably wondering where we at." "Okay well hopefully this will help me locate Bryk. Thanks everyone. I'll keepyou posted." The officer says, standing.

Diana consoles Haddie as they all stand up to leave. "You still aint heard from them, either?" Haddie asks.

"Naw, not yet Ma. Snake either. I left them all a voice message and a text."

CHAPTER 32

Sli, Big Sheddy, Felanie and Streng drive around looking for the best location to bury Tawny. Felanie turns on the radio. "Mind Blowing Decisions" by Heatwave plays. Felanie sings along with it: "'...*Taking my time to work the problem out yet trying to convince her that there is no need for doubt. Mind blowing decisions 'cause it's head on collision.*'" "Heeey! This my skating jaaaam!" She says, swaying to the beat, as she turns up the volume.

Sli turns the music off. "What are you tryna get us busted? Go where we went last time. But this time try to stay on the side streets as much as you can 'cause you know the pigs and they grannies lurking this time a mornin'."

Felanie drives in and out of one-way side streets until she has no choice but to turn onto a busy intersection. Just as she is approaching a traffic light, the lights on a police car begins flashing behind them.

"Aaaaw shit! Did you have the turn signal on?" Sli asks "Of course!"

"Giiirrrl...you bet not fuck this up!" Sli says through gritted teeth.

Felanie turns her head slowly, raising her eyebrows, as she glares at Sli. "No, the fuck you didn't just say that!"

CHAPTER 33

A doctor walks into the family's waiting room accompanied by Nurse Jersie and a police officer. They both approach Bruno. The doctor extends his hand and introduces himself. "I am extremely sorry for all the confusion. The officer was just showing us a picture of your son, Bryk. I believe I am the one who worked on him when he first arrived. I can explain why he was brought in." Family members and relatives start coming closer to listen to the conversation.

"Are you okay with us talking here or would you like a private room?" The doctor asks. "Aw naw. This cool right here, doc. Know what I'm sayin'." Bruno says as he adjusts himself in his seat.

"Okay…so…apparently…Bryk suffered severe burns due to an excessive fireworks explosion." Gasping, and other type of pleadings for the Lord's mercy can be heard from the people listening.

The police officer steps up to stand beside the doctor to speak. "And this is another reason why I was called in to investigate. Apparently, according to the medical record, Bryk's burns are extensive and was caused by explosives that are illegal in Illinois under the PUA— Pyrotechnic Use Act. A person convicted of PUA will be looking at as much as a year in prison and a twenty-five hundred dollar fine. And again, because your son is a minor, I need to know how he got access to such explosives? And if he isn't responsible for his own injuries then I need to investigate to find out whois?"

Bruno covers his face with his hands, softly sobbing. He then wipes his eyes and nose with the palms of his hands and wrists. An extended string of snot stays connected to his wrist. He uses an index finger to disconnect it then wipes it on his pants. Someone throws him a napkin, but it lands on the floor.

"Wait…What's really going on? I don't know nothing about none of this. How…What happened? Know what I mean? So, you say he sleep now?" Bruno asks, between sniffles, continuing to wipe his face with his hands. "So, this means you know which room he's in?" He snatches the napkin from the floor to clean his face and hands.

"We don't have specific details. But I can assure you he was not in any pain because he was unconscious when he arrived...Mr. Townsmend. You know what? You've already gone through enough. So, let me check again to make absolutely sure we have the right person and in which room exactly. I'll be right back," The doctor says, then quickly walks away.

"To be or not to be." Bruno mumbles softly. "That is the question. Whether 'tis nobler in the mind to suffer the slings and arrows of outrageous fortune. Or to take arms against a sea of troubles..."

Diana, who is sitting next to Bruno, turns her head slowly, staring and listening intently, her face grimaces. "Da fuck! Dude...you chanting Shakespeare?"

Bruno looks at Diana, then avert his gaze to the floor. "Yeeeah... You know what I'm sayin'...it's like my prayer and shit." And by opposing end them. To die to sleep..." Bruno continues.

"Damn! Yous a fuckin' retard. Nooooow I see why Sli left yo' dumb ass. Let me get the hell on away from here." Diana jumps from her seat, walking quickly, damn near running away.

CHAPTER 34

Officer One walks over to the driver's side of the pickup truck. He points a flashlight inside. Officer Two stands on the passenger's side, looking around, anxious and fidgety.

"Turn off the ignition." Officer One says. "Is there a problem officer?" Felanie asks.

"I'll tell you that once I'm more acquainted with ya. Now slowly hand over your license and registration."

Felanie leans, sloth-like slowly, toward the glove compartment. Officer One widens his eyes. "Oh, you tryna fuck with me right now?" "No, no, no sir. I don't want nooomisunderstandings."

"You gotta gun in there or something? Officer One doesn't wait for an answer as he snatches the gun from his holster. Officer Two follows suit.

"Holon now!" Sli yells

"Whoa, whoa, whoa!" Big Sheddy yells. "Aw hell naw!" Felanie shouts in disbelief.

"Wha da fuuu…" Streng loudly screams his usual form of protest.

"You're all gonna slowly step outta the vehicle. Leave the headlights on. Sit on the curb in front of the truck and spread-out arm's length apart." Officer One barks commands, standing with his feet spread apart and both hands on his gun, aiming at Felanie's head.

CHAPTER 35

A doctor and police officer return to the waiting room. The doctor stands in front of Bruno, looking down at him, and says, "Mr. Townsmend we've located Bryk." Everyone turns to look at him. The doctor sits down beside Bruno. "As I stated before, he was burned pretty badly from fireworks. The paramedics had to administer CPR on him during the ride in the ambulance. They got him stabilized, but he flat lined again not long after he arrived here." The doctor places a hand on Bruno's shoulder. "Unfortunately, he didn't make it." Murmurings, high pitched screaming and wailing sound out as the doctor continue, "I want to assure you we did everything we could…"

Bruno knocks the doctor's hand from his shoulder then quickly stands up. "OOOH MY GAAAWD! I hope those gangs ain't did nothin' to my boy. I swear to God! I know somebody saw sumthin' though." He turns around slowly. "IS THERE ANYBODY IN HERE WHO WAS AT GARFIELD PARK? OR IF YOU KNOW WHO WAS, CALL THEY ASSES UP NOW!"

CHAPTER 36

As Sli, Felanie, Streng and Big Sheddy sit on the curb, Officer One, who is standing behind them, radios in for backup.

Sli turns to look behind her. "Officer there's no need for backup. We're just working on making some repairs to my mom's house. We were on our way…"

"Shut the fuck up!" Officer One yells. "Yes sir."

Officer Two searches the pickup truck as Officer One paces back and forth. Sli's phone begins ringing. "May I please answer this officer? My son was rushed to the emergency room earlier."

"Obviously, you can't tell the difference between a priest's robe and a cop's uniform. I'm not interested in your sob ass stories," Officer One says. He kneels behind Sli and points his gun to her temple. "Go ahead and answer it but don't try nothing stupid."

"Thanks officer." Sli says then answers her phone. …Yeah, so what's going on?"

There's wailing in the background. "They finally found Bryk in the morgue!" Diana musters between sobs. She cries before continuing to speak. "They couldn't even find him at first. Now they're telling us he's dead, Sli! You, Snake and the twins need to get here now! Yall should've been here already! Where is you at?" Sli's eyes go into a blank stare as she drops the phone.

Sirens are approaching. Three cop cars come to a screeching halt. Officers get out their vehicles, standing around.

Streng is looking down at the ground when Officer One decides to stand on top of his shoes. Streng looks up with confusion at the officer.

"So, what's with all those two by fours?" The officer asks.

When Streng doesn't respond, Officer One puts more pressure onto his toes. Streng's face grimaces in pain, when he quickly looks over at Sli for answers.

Sli appears dazed and doesn't even notice what is happening at first. Seconds pass before she turns to look at them and respond in a trancelike tone. "He's hearing-impaired officer."

Officer One looks at Sli with disdain. "Bitch! Am I standing on your shoes?" Sli doesn't respond.

"You feeling left out or something?" Sli still doesn't respond.

Officer One continues grinding the soles of his shoes along the top of Streng's feet. "Oooooow! What the fuuu'!" Streng yells.

Officer Two peeks from behind the pickup truck and yells, "Yo Moretti!" Moretti, Officer One, quickly looks at Officer Two. "We got a live one back here. Sounds likethese dumb fucks botched up a hit." Officer Two says chuckling. "Someone's…yelling…for help… from these sticks!" He manages to say stillchuckling.

All the officers draw their guns toward Sli, Big Sheddy, Streng andFelanie. "Put your hands above your…" Officer Morettisays.

"Officer…no it's not…" Sli says.

Shots ring out. Everybody dives to the ground. Officer Moretti falls slowly and lands flat on his face between Streng and Sli.

Streng quickly grabs the handcuff key from the fallen officer before everyone is back in an upright position. Sli and Felanie sees him.

CHAPTER 37

An orderly is pushing Nicky into the emergency room, in a wheelchair, when she overhears Bruno's ranting. Nicky's clothes are tattered, and her hair is an unkempt mess of a partially matted afro, resembling a bird's nest, as it sets adjacent to partially braided extensions. Her face grimaces as if Bruno's questions personally offend her.

The orderly parks the wheelchair near a wall, locking the brakes. Various people respond to Bruno's question with a no, naw or shaking their heads. Bruno sighs so loudly it resembles a roar. He sits down, then lays his head on his folded arms across his knees. People console him.

Bruno jumps up again. "Come on yall…Yall need to be calling around and asking…I JUST NEED ANSWERS…SOMEBODY GOTTA KNOW WHAT HAPPENED TO MY BOY!" He passes out, falling hard on the edge of his chair, before sliding to the floor.

CHAPTER 38

Officer Two shouts into his walkie talkie that Officer Moretti has been shot. As he and the other officers run to check on him, more police cars are pulling up, along with the paramedics.

"Secure this area. Make sure not another car can drive through here from, at least, miles away," Officer Two yells, then turns to the officer standing closest to him. "Keep a close watch on these motherfuckers. I believe they set us up!"

"NO…NO…NO! Sir we did not set you up!" Sli pleads.

Officer Two looks around. "I need some of you to get those two by fours from the back of that truck. Somebody was in there yelling for help earlier…if they haven't died by now!"

Officer Two walks over to Sli. "Lying bitch!" He punches her in the face.

Sli's head swings to one side. She spits out blood. "Man, I'd be a damned fool to set you up when I'm sittin' right here not able to defend my own mufuckin' self!"

Officer Two dives on Sli, knocking her backward, pressing his knee into her stomach and strangling her. "Oh, you wanna get smart now bitch. Who were you talkin' to on the phone?"

Sli is gasping for air as tears fall from her eyes. Officer Two removes his hands from her neck but remains leaning on her stomach. Sli twists her body so that Officer Two's knee hits the concrete. Sli is bawled in a fetal position. Officer Two leans his elbow into Sli's shoulder. "Man, that was my sister." She says between groans. "They claim they found my son dead in the hospital."

Officer Two points his finger in Sli's face. "You better not be fucking lying," he says before standing up and limping away.

Sli sits up, holding her stomach, then rubbing her neck and shoulders. She looks at Streng but is really talking to herself. "How da fuck you find a dead body in a hospital morgue?" Streng scrunches his eyebrows and turns up his lips as Sli continues speaking without bothering to explain. "You supposed to know who you have before taking them to the morgue. So, it sounds like they tryna say my boy died alone as a John fucking Doe…" Sli looks away, vigorously shaking her head, softly crying. "Aw man this is one fucked up situation." She then looks angrily into nowhere. "Naw! This some bullshit! Fuck that! That aint nona my son they found dead." She looks back at Streng with lifted eyebrows, slowly stressing each word. *I-gotta-go-find-my- son.*

Officer Two returns and squats to make direct eye contact with Sli. "And is this semi dead body like a retaliation for *your dead son*?" Sli hangs her head.

"I thought so…Guilty as fuck," Officer Two says with disdain. "Naw, naw, naw. Officer it's not like that," Sli says.

More sirens approach then go silent as lights continue flashing. Officer Two stands and turns his head to speak to another officer. "Book these shitheads! Put 'em all in the paddy wagon." Officers Three and Four rough up Felanie, Streng, Sli and Big Sheddy to get them on their feet.

Officer Two directs his attention to another officer. "What's the word on the body in the sticks?" Officer Two continues a conversation with another officer when Officer Three yells out. "Hey! They're not even in handcuffs? Somebody's slippin'!"

"I was saving something for you to do." Officer Two yells back. "Wait! Can I go pee furst I gotta go weelly ba'." Streng asks.

"Why da fuck's he talking like Elmer Fudd?" Officer Three asks as he grabs Streng by the top of his T-shirt and shoves him toward a port-o-potty. Officers Three and Four burst up laughing.

"Sounds like he's deaf, dumb, or both or some shit." Officer four butts in. Streng goes into the port-o-potty while Officer three waits outside.

The other officers are handcuffing Big Sheddy, Sli and Felanie as they stand in front of a police car.

The port-o-potty door flies open as Streng sprints full speed down the street.

"Hey! Get back here! Perp's getting away!" Officer three yells as he chases Streng.

While everyone is looking toward the commotion, Felanie and Sli break out running in different directions.

CHAPTER 39

People run toward Bruno, helping him back into his seat. One person fans him, with a limp, disassembled newspaper. Once the semi-crowd scatters to their various areas, a pale priest, with his hands folded in front of his chin, stands before Bruno. The priest's burnt-orange shoulder length curly hair is tucked behind his ears, He swings his head from side to side—as if removing hair from his face, but none is. "Hello my brotha Bruno." Bruno is leaning to one side of his seat, but sits up quickly, and knocks the fanning newspaper from the fanner's hands. He gazes confusedly at the priest. "Dude, I understand you lost your son." The priest continues, still swinging his head. "I was called here in case you would like for me to help you with the sacrament of penance."

Bruno, doubly confused, jerks his head back. Someone, standing behind the priest, raises up on their tippy toes, the priest leans to one side, making it easier for the unseen person to whisper into his ear. The priest nods his head, then continues speaking. "Anyway, dude, you have my deepest condolences. Actually, dude, I stand corrected. I was called here in case you would like prayer."

"I already prayed." Bruno replies.

Again, the person behind the priest whispers in his ear. "Okay… very well dude…in that case…may I fetch you a cup of wat…"

"NOBODY MOVE! NOBODY GETS HURT! PUT YALL MUTHAFUCKIN' HANDS

UP!" Everybody looks in the direction of the door. It's Sli. She shoots her gun toward the ceiling. A light shatter as debris falls around her. Everyone screams and duck.

Felanie has the fat security officer in a sleep hold. Streng is shifting the aim of his gun in different directions as he glances around the room.

"Mama! Where you at?" Sli yells.

Bruno's mouth and eyes are wide open as he stands up slowly. Others look on in total shock. Sli walks slowly toward the family while continuing to look around the room. She points the gun into a doctor's face. "Dude! You look like you wanna try somethin' stupid. I will end your life." Sli swiftly glance around the room. "As a matter of fact, er'body lay on the muthafuckin flo!"

Bruno has a sly grin on his face as he gawks at Sli, lustfully licking his lips. "Yo ass is lookin' fuckin' sexy right about now though." His mood changes to irritation once he realizes what's really happening. "But what da fuck is you doin' right now, Sli?" Bruno snaps.

"Where my son at, Bruno?" "I thought they told you…"

"I did!" Diana, cuts Bruno off, while mean mugging Sli. With clenched teeth, Diana jumps up and rushes toward Sli. "I already tolchu where Bryk at."

Sli points the gun at Diana. "If you don't get the fuck out my face." Diana jerks her head back.

"Sli what the fuck is you doin'?" Haddie says, standing, placing her hands on her hips.

"Have you done lost yo' whole got damn mind?"

The security officer is still struggling to break free as Felanie continues her grip around his neck.

"Dude, you must not know what the hell you doin' cause he shoulda been sleep by now." Nicky blurts out.

"I'm floundering puttin' this mufucka out. It's like he's a fraternal twin to a whale." Felanie replies.

Nicky turns to look at another person. "You know what I'm sayin'?" She looks back at Felanie. "At the rate you going you gone be puttin' that big mufuka to sleep fa da rest of yo' life."

Sli lowers her gun as she walks closer to Bruno. "Did any of yall even look to see who the person in the morgue really was 'cause I know it's not my son."

Haddie stares at Sli, shaking her head in disbelief. "I always figured you had some sort of death wish on yo'self, but this just confirms it."

Haddie, squinting her eyes, points her hands at her temples. "Do you *not* realize whatchu doin' right now?"

There's a knock at the automatic doors. "Sli, it's Snake." Streng announces. "Let him in."

Streng unlocks the door. Snake rushes over to the family. "What's goin' on?" He notices Sli is holding a gun. "Da fuck is yo problem, Sli?"

"Yo kids is my muthafukin problem!"

"The fuck is you talkin 'bout? Bryk's death aint got nothin' to do with my kids?" Snake looks around. "Where my kids at?" Snake asks panicked. He walks toward Haddie. "Mama yall all right? What's going on? Where the twins?" They talk softly among themselves.

Nicky sits back chuckling to herself. "Ha! Mama say her daughter, crazy ass, gotta death wish. Ya got that right, Mama, 'cause she is goin' out execution style, soon as those pigs arrive." Nicky yells.

Sli does a double take as she looks at Nicky. "Nicky? What the hell…The fuck happened to you?" Sli asks.

"Who that is?" Nicky asks.

"You that fucked up?" Sli squints. "You got brain damage? It's Sli!"

"Giiirlfriend! I thought that sounded like you! Wait! Is that you for real, Sli? It does kind of sound like you. eI aint got my contacts in so I can't see good. But anyway, one of my tricks got stupid and thought he was gonna get away without paying me. Shiiiit! You think I'm fucked up? You should see that fat funky fucker…"

There's another knock on the sliding glass doors. Sli quickly points her gun in that direction. Everybody's head turns in that direction. It's an elderly man and woman looking to get medical attention. Sli slowly directs her gun around the room. "Nobody better try nothin' crazy!" She says walking toward the automatic door. She points her gun back and forth, into each of the elderly stranger's faces. They are stunned, stumbling over one another, before hobbling away as Sli returns to where she was standing.

"Sli please don't end up in jail or dead after all this cause you gotta freshen up my 'do. I tolchu it's almost time for my full transition and

I gotta keep gettin' those bangin' hairstyles 'cause I must look good in order to keep makin' my stash." Nicky chuckles, sticks out her tongue, swings her hands around in the air, dancing in her wheelchair. Stopping abruptly, she pleads with Sli. "So just get us out of here alive. But Girl! If you gotta another gun I cooould help you though."

Sli rolls her eyes and smacks her lips.

Streng is grinning widely as he continues watching Felanie still struggling to put the security officer to sleep. "Man, you makin' that shit hawda than necessawee. Just knoc' dat big mufucka out witcho piece. Oops…sorry Ms.Haddie."

"Just shut the fuck up, Streng!" Felanieshouts.

The security officer finally drifts off to sleep. Felanie struggles getting the handcuffs from under him.

Sli looks at Haddie. "Ma, I aint crazy and I sho aint the one with a death wish."

Haddie shakes her head. Tears begin forming in her eyes. "Sli, now you gotta know that was the wrong answer in front of all these damn people. Don't you realize you need to be fallin' out and foamin' at the mouth right about now 'cause that may be yo' only chance of not joinin' yo' son in the that morgue."

"My son aint in no morgue!" Sli says, stomping her feet.

There's loud banging on the automatic doors. "Streng keep yo' eyes and yo gun on these mufukas. Looks like I gotta break it down better to get these muthafukas to scram!"

Sli gets to the automatic doors and sees there are two paramedics and a patient on a gurney. One of the paramedics is mouthing words that are muffled but still audible. "We need you to let us in. This young lady could die if she doesn't receive medical attention immediately."

Sli looks at the patient and recognizes it's Tawny. Tawny is looking back at Sli with one eye barely open as the other one is swollen shut.

CHAPTER 40

More cop cars and another ambulance arrive on the scene. Officer Two has his gun drawn on Big Sheddy as he sits handcuffed in the back of a police truck. "Okay tubby you need to talk fast." Officer Two says as he wipes sweat from his forehead and neck with his hand. "Where are your buddies heading now?"

"Ion even know osifa. And you can call me Big Sheddy though." Officer Two slaps Big Sheddy.

"Stop fucking with me Big Shitty before I put a bullet in yo' barrel shaped ass."

"But osifa...you really think I'll sit here riskin' my life for those dumb mufuckas? Hell naw! If I knew I'd be singing like a canary...for real osifa."

"Oh yeah? Okay you inflated stool pigeon. We'll see about that. What's the young lady's name who you thought you were about to bury in those sticks?"

"Whatchu mean? You sayin' you found somebody dead in some sticks, osifa? Now ion know nothin' 'bout..."

Officer Two slaps him harder this time. When Big Sheddy's head returns to face him, Officer Two leans in closer to look him in the eyes. "Okay now you Listen up you bat fastard...You're looking at life in prison for attempted murder. Now if you're excited about getting a dooky shoot stretched as huge as your ankles so you would have to plug it up with a whole pair of your own pants to stop from shittin' your drawers every second..."

"Ooooooh you talkin' bout Sli's niece, Tawny. Sli fucked her up real bad 'cause she said Tawny stole her stuff. We tried to tell Sli she was takin' shit too far but she was all like 'Fuck family!'" Big Sheddy's voice goes high pitched in an attempt at mocking Sli. "So, when Tawny finally fell over bleedin' and shit, we thought she was dead. So, Sli was all like 'Clean this shit up'..." Big Sheddy mocks Sli again.

Officer Two beckons his hand to get someone's attention. A paramedic walks over. Big Sheddy continues talking although no one is listening. "So that's when we went in the backyard to make the casket out of two by fours. They house only a few minutes from here…"

Officer Two whispers into the paramedic's ear. "We got our informant. Tranquilize this bulldozer before he tries to roll away. I'm gonna go help track down the other fugitives."

Big Sheddy looks at his fingernails. "I don't know the exact address but it's like about the seventh duplex apartment building from the corner in the 2700 block on Monroe Street. So, if you heading north on California Ave, just hang a left…" Big Sheddy continues talking long after the officer walks away and until the paramedic sedateshim.

CHAPTER 41

Sli is disappointed to see Tawny lying on the gurney, so she quickly points the gun at the paramedics. "Go find another hospital to take her to. Now get the fuck away from the door!" Sli walks back toward the middle of the room.

Nicky looks back and forth between Sli and Haddie before speaking. "Mama you sho telling Sli right 'cause befo' this is finished we may all end up takin' a dirt nap."

Sli rubs her temples, the gun still in her hand. "Nicky, just shut the fuck up!"

Haddie is shaking her head profusely. "Naw baby. I'm not gettin' caught up in nona this bullshit. I aint dying or going to jail for nobody. Not even my own kids!" Haddie yells toward Sli but is responding to Nicky.

"Mama, please stop!" Sli yells.

"Sli, just think about what a mess you making and how your life is gonna change after all this. So, you need to just stop…"

"STOOOP! SHHHH…Mama STOP agreeing with them. Yall not listening to me. Don't believe the hype. My son is not dead. They put him in there and aint none of yall seen him first. Nona yall even know if it's really him 'cause nobody even bothered tocheck."

Nicky uses her feet to scoot herself forward in the wheelchair. "Whew! I'm so glad I'm starting to feel so much better. I can go home now." Once she gets about ten feet from the wall, she stands up and starts walking away.

Sli points the gun at Nicky. Nicky throws her hands up, screaming. "Nicky, go sit yo' ass back down!" Sli yells.

Nicky screams again, turns around and runs back to sit down in the wheelchair. "I can't believe you just did that shit to me!" Nicky's shoulders slumps as she takes a deep breath and releases it quickly. "I was on yo damn side." Nicky semi-whispers.

The knock is harder at the automatic door. Sli turns to look. A paramedic yells out. "The patient is losing consciousness. Please… at least just let her in. We'll stay out here, and you can let a doctor take care of her." The paramedic holds up a paper. "Here's is all the information doctor needs to know about the patient."

"Felanie, pull that gurney in…Streng, keep the gun on the medics…" Sli says then turns the gun toward the doctor. He cowers. "You will take care of her right out here." Sli says as the gurney is pulled toward them.

The doctor puts the stethoscope on Tawny's chest while asking, "What's your name sweetheart."

"Tawny Maldive." Snake, Haddie and Diana all look in Tawny's direction in shock then rushes over to her.

"Tawny? Baby…What happened to you." Snake asks shaken up.

With her one good eye, Tawny slowly turns her head to look in Sli's direction.

Snake looks angrily at Sli, then gets in her face. "You did this to my baby…Your own fucking niece? Where the fuck is my son? What did you do to him? Huh, Sli?"

Sli steps back and points the gun at Snake. "Get outta my face." Everyone gasps.

"I'm gonna need everyone to please calm down and step back." The doctor says. He then addresses Sli. "Listen lady I can't take care of her out here. She may have internal damages and the only way to find that out is if she has x-rays or even other tests. You're gonna have to let me take her in a room where there are proper supplies."

"You bitch! You hurt my baby like this. Yo' own flesh and blood?" Snake says as he is charging at Sli but Diana and Haddie hold him back. "So, did you kill my son since your son is dead!" Snake breaks free from Haddie and Diana, charging toward Sli.

Sli shoots. Snake falls to the ground. Everyone screams and duck.

"Snake!" Haddie yells as she and Diana rushes toward him.

CHAPTER 42

Tyler is sleeping, fully dressed on the couch, with the game controller resting loosely in his hand. He is awakened by a rapidly ringing doorbell and loud banging on the exterior door. "Police! Is anybody in there? Open up or we're busting the door down!"

Tyler walks downstairs and opens it. Policemen barge in with their guns drawn. "Who else is here with you?" The officer asks.

Tyler's eyes are just as wide open as his mouth.

CHAPTER 43

Haddie is on her knees, alternating between comforting Snake and looking up at Sli with rage and disgust. "I cannot believe you are my child right now. You are acting sincerely sick in the head! You would rather try to kill your own niece and twin brother than to let go of that stubbornness. What's going on with you, child?"

"Oh my God, Mama! He's still breathing so it can't be that bad. The doc'll put a band aid on it, and he'll be just fine." Sli says as she rolls her eyes and waves her wrist, flinging the gun in different directions before pointing it at a doctor. "Hey you, doc! Come get him and patch him up. Put him in the room with his daughter." Sli says as shechuckles.

Sirens and screeching car tires along with flashing siren lights are heard and seen outside the emergency department. "This is the Chicago Police Department. This hostage situation needs to end now!" An officer announces through a megaphone. "Come out with your hands in the air!"

Nicky exaggeratedly flails her arms and hands around and slaps her lap, "See now...Gaaawd daaaamn it, Sli!" Nicky rolls her neck as she moves her head in different directions, making sounds of exasperation, while smacking her lips. "Now my hair aint never gon' get done. Who else imma find cheaper than you?"

Sli points her gun at nurse Jersie. "Now take me to my real son, who I know is still breathing."

CHAPTER 44

Brandon returns to Snake's Auto. The darkness of the windows makes the shop appear to be closed. He turns the knob. It's locked so he knocks. He cuffs his hand to his face as he looks closer into the window of the door, then through the picture window next to it. He sees a figure then knocks harder.

Odeo is wiping his hands when he hears knocking. He sees it's Brandon and walks over to open it. "May I help jou?" Odeo asks, while remaining in the doorway.

"Man, I'm checking on my car. I've been calling all day but nobody's answering the phone. Where's Snake?

"Jou know 'bout as much as I do." Odeo replies.

"Maaan…What's that supposed to mean?" Brandon says as he pushes his way through the door.

"Hey! I haven't seen him. No one was here when I got here" Odeo humps his shoulders. "So, I know how to let myself in and dat's all I know."

"Man, Where's my car?" Odeo points to Brandon's car. Brandon walks over to it. "So, what's going on with it? Is it fixed?" Brandon asks.

Odeo humps his shoulders. "Fuck if I know, but I doubt it."

Brandon shifts his body weight and rolls his eyes. "Have the parts even come in yet?" "Snake would know. But since he aint here I don't know no'ting eitha."

"So, you haven't heard anything from him?"

"Man, I just said…My English that bad to jou…No?"

"Look man, I don't know what's going on. But could you make my car your priority. I needed it like weeks ago." Brandon goes in his wallet and gives Odeo his business card. "Here's my number. He called me and said a part is in, but he was still waiting for the other part. Could you check now to see if the parts came in yet?"

Odeo leaves to go check. Minutes later he returns. "Dey're bof rightchere." He holds up a package in his hands.

"If you could get it to me by the end of the day, I'd appreciate it." Brandon says. "The customer's car I'm working on now feels zactly like jou…"

"Yeah, yeah understood." Brandon goes back into his wallet and gives Odeo a hundred- dollar bill.

"Cool. I'll have it ready for jou this evening." Odeo assures him with a big grin. His golden tooth glistens.

"Thanks bro!" Brandon says as he puts up his fist. They fist bump and Brandon leaves. The grin slowly leaves Odeo face as he stares at Brandon until he walks out of sight.

CHAPTER 45

Snake is in a patient's room where a doctor has just bandaged his wound. "Well Mr. Maldive that could have been a whole lot worse. Thankfully the bullet just grazed you. It went through several layers of skin, but it didn't touch any vital arteries or shatter any bones." The doctor stands near the trash bin, removing and dropping his gloves into it. "But despite the tension we're under right now you're gonna have to stay calm and don't do anything to overwork that arm. The last thing we want is for it to start bleeding again…." The doctor places a hand on Snake's healthy arm to get him to look into his eyes. "Am I understanding it correctly that that's your twin sister who could've killed you?" Snake nods. "Wow! Talk about sibling rivalry. I know I've intentionally pissed my sisters off because I enjoy doing it. But you all havetaken family feud…How my kids say it…? to a whole nother vortex." The doctor chuckles and shakes his head.

Snake is gazing in a daydream. "Doc I assure you I didn't do a damn thang to her. I've told her she bugs out over the stupidest stuff. But this time it *is* a big deal 'cause she don't wanna face the fact that her son is dead." Snake snaps out of his daydream stare and squints at the doctor. "You know what I'm sayin'…"

The doctor raises his eyebrows and nods. "Oh yeah, I overstand."

"Uh listen doc, I don't wanna stay back here. Can I go back out in the waiting area?" "Weeeellll, not just yet. It's best if you stay back here and try to relax. Besides your sister may decide to take another shot and you may not be so lucky next time."

"Naw doc. That's not gonna happen. As long as those fools holding guns on er'body they subject to kill each other first. That's why I'd rather be in that waiting area 'cause my Mama and li' sister out there and I'd feel better if I could be there to watch out for them. I promise to still relax out there."

The doctor scrunches his face and shakes his head. "I understand how you feel. But you must take care of yourself first. That wound is still at risk of getting infected, which is why I've prescribed you some antibiotics to take once you get home."

Snake hangs his head for a few seconds then looks up again. "Okay…Well can I at least see my daughter?" The doctor takes a while to respond. "Please doc. Seeing my baby like that really tore me up inside. I would really like to see her so I can assure her that everything is going to be okay. I know she's terrified."

"Okay but only after you promise me, you'll come right back in here and rest." "I promise, doc." Snake eases himself slowly out of bed.

The doctor washes his hand then dries them with paper towels as he stands in the doorway, facing the nurse's desk. "Nurse, could you see to it that Mr. Maldive visits his daughter for only a few minutes. Then make sure he returns right back here to lie down."

"Sure thing." The nurse agrees.

The doctor nods at Snake as he exits the room.

CHAPTER 46

Sli and Nurse Jersie takes the elevator for medical staff only. "Now Ms. Maldive I need you to understand…I cannot take you directly into the morgue. You'll have to wait outside. The way it works is it'll show a picture of your son on the monitor, which is displayed through the win…"

"Shut the fuck up. I'll decide how this is gonna go once we're down there." Sli presses the gun against Nurse Jersie's temple. "And bitch…I *swear*…don't try to get slick either."

As they exit the elevator Sli firmly embraces her gun, as she points it toward nurse Jersie, who nervously enters the code to unlock the door. "I swear fo' God… You bringing me down here like you convinced that's my son dead in there. If it is or if it aint I'm killing you."

"Again, Ms. Maldive, I need to remind you that this room is highly infectious with all manner of bacteria. I'm going to put your son's picture up on the monitor so you can see him through this window." Nurse Jersie says, pointing to the window next to the door.

Sli walks up to Nurse Jersie, points the gun on top of her head, and whispers: "And, bitch, I need to remind you, whatever the case may be, I will write your name across this entire glass window in your blood and brains. Got it?" Nurse Jersie nods rapidly.

Stepping inside the room, Nurse Jersie hits the light switch. Sli stands in the doorway. Nurse Jersie quickly turns around, placing her hand up near Sli's chest. "Please, Sli, for your own protection it's best you stand outside the door."

Sli looks down and sees a wooden doorstop. "Put that thing in the door so it won't close all the way." Sli demands.

Nurse Jersie obliges, then disappears behind a wall.

Seconds go by. "What's going on? What's taking so long?" Sli yells out. "I have to wear protection back here."

"Well, hell I could've done that too." Sli says.

"I'm almost done." Nurse Jersie partially stands from behind the wall while putting slippers over her shoes. "Trust me there's a whole lot more to this place than you could ever want to know about." Nurse Jersie' eyes soften. She steps out, putting her mask over her face, as she thinks of what she could say next. "Your son's open wounds are certainly a health risk so…"

"THAT AINT NONE OF MY SON, GODDAMNIT!"

Nurse Jersie's eyes widen, throwing her hands up. "Oh…Okay…" she points toward the back. "I'm about to go on back now."

Seconds later the monitor light comes on and a picture of Bryk's face pops up. Sli screams. Bending over in anguish, she grabs the wall to avoid falling.

Nurse Jersie slams the door and quickly turns out the lights. The only thing still illuminated is Bryk's picture. Sli continues screaming and crying uncontrollably.

CHAPTER 47

Snake sits in a chair next to his daughter's bed. Tears well in eyes as he is made to look at her swollen and discolored face. "Listen baby...I am so sorry you had to go through this mess with yo crazy ass auntie. What was her so called reason for doing this to you?" Snake asks wrestling to contain his anger.

Tawny takes a deep breath. "She was saying I stole her stuff. Daddy, I didn't even touch her stuff. I...

"It's okay baby. I know you didn't. Exactly what did she do to you?"

"She tied me to a chair and hit me with a bag of bricks."

Tears fall from Snake's eyes. He slowly rubs his hand down his face, which contorts into raging anger. "Bag of bricks?"

"Yeah...She had Big Sheddy go get the bricks. I heard Felanie trying to stop her, but she wouldn't listen."

"Who else was there helping her?"

"Streng. They must've knocked me out because when I woke up, I was wrapped in plastic, and it was dark. I was so scared. I was screaming and banging and kicking. I didn't know where I was. Then I heard the police, and they took forever to get me out."

Snake nods, watching how upset she was getting, made him feel even more helpless. "You have nothing more to worry about, baby girl. I promise you that."

"What happened to your arm, daddy. Did she hurt you too?"

"Don't you worry about me, baby. I'm gonna be fine. You the one who need to get well and be outta here. So, *you* can keep whooping ass in chess. We gotta get you in that tournament."

A nurse walks into the room to check Tawny's IV monitor and vitals. "I'm sorry Mr.

Maldive, but your doctor said to make sure you get back to your room so that the both of you can rest up."

Snake nods. "So, what's going on with my baby, nurse?"

"So far all we can see from the x-rays is a concussion. It looks as if there may be some hemorrhaging on the brain, but we won't be a hundred percent sure until after the MRI andCT Scan results return. Those tests will also show if there are any other internaldamages."

Snake wipes his eyes before more tears fall. He stands and places a hand gently on top of Tawny's head. "I wanna hug you so bad but I don't wanna do you any more damage. You get plenty of rest baby and hurry up and get the hell outta here so you can fail again at kicking my butt in another game of hoops."

Tawny smiles weakly. Snake stares at her a while before bending to gently kiss her on the cheek.

"I love you baby."
"I love you too daddy."
Snake walks out. Tawny drifts off to sleep.

CHAPTER 48

Sli exits the elevator. Walking swiftly, with fury in her eyes, throughout the hospital corridors.

****

Snake walks swiftly, with fury in his eyes, throughout the hospital corridors. He arrives in the emergency room waiting area. He walks right up to Streng, snatches his gun and points it at Felanie. "Yo big ass gotta know this shit ends right now!" He points the gun back and forth between Streng and Felanie.

"Both yall muthafukas helped that bitch fuck my baby up like that. You know it's about time for me to return the favor right...YOU BITCH ASS NIGGAS!"

Snake shoots the ceiling, debris falls. People scream and duck. Snake points his gun shakily at Felanie. "Lay yo shit on the flo and kick it to me."

Felanie does it. When Snake bends down to pick up the gun, Sli steps on it. Snake looks up. Sli has her gun pointed at his head. Snake stands slowly then swiftly points his gun back at Sli. Everyone is watching in terror.

"Now you know this could only go one of two ways. I'm either gonna put another serious hurting on ya or you might just die this time." Sli says.

"Bitch, you tried to kill my daughter! Yo own *niece?*" Snake's tone is an octave higher as he's half stating half questioning in disbelief. "But you done fucked up by not taking me out when you had the chance, 'cause you won't get another one to do nothin' else to nan nother one of us. Now I swear you better tell me what you did to my son?"

Sli doesn't respond. "Where my son at, Sli!"

Haddie jumps up from her chair. "Yall need to stop this crazy shit! Right now!" Snake and Sli continue staring each other down. Haddie slowly walks over to them and stands next to Snake. "I swear fo God yall better put those fucking guns down! Now! Sli, do you know where Tyler is?"

Sli looks at Haddie. "No."

As more police cars pull up from every direction outside the emergency room, sirens die as lights continue flashing. Various news reporters and camera crews are setting up their equipment, testing their microphones.

"Sli Maldive and anyone else who is holding a gun, this is your second warning." An officer announces through a megaphone. "Come out with your hands up!"

Felanie walks over to the gun on the floor and picks it up by the barrel. Snake points his gun at her. Felanie gently places her gun in Haddie's hand.

Sli looks at Felanie with confusion, then anger. "The fuck is you doing? Oooh it's like that huh, Felanie? After all the shit I did for you."

Felanie walks away.

CHAPTER 49

Brandon walks into Snake's office. Odeo, with a smirk on his face, sits with his feet propped up on Snake's desk, looking up at the mounted television.

"Man, sorry I'm late and thanks for waiting around. I'm trying to stay away from using any more credit cards." Brandon says, shuffling the cash he's counting.

"Aw man now jou know that's no problemo. Jou're one of our faithful, no haggling customers. Aint that how yo boy Snake say?"

"Speaking of him…You still haven't heard from him yet?" Brandon asks.

Odeo grins, displaying his gold teeth. "Yeah, I found him. He's right there." He points up at the television. Brandon looks up to see the words BREAKING NEWS flashing on the screen.

"We're here at Cook County Hospital, where apparently a hostage situation is taking place. Sources are saying it appears to be a stand off between a set of brother and sister twins. Further details are yet unknown…"

Brandon stares with his mouth open. "What the fuck? So, Snake is being held hostage at the hospital?"

"Ha! Dat mudderfuka should be so lucky. Sounds like him and his seester the perps holding people hostage." Odeo says.

"What? Why though?" Brandon asks Odeo humps his shoulders. "Ell if I know, man. Imma find out though. But it looks like he won't be running this shop for a while, heh?"

"Oh, that aint all he won't be doing for a while." Brandon agrees.

Odeo takes his feet from the desk and leans his elbows on it. "Look here…I overhear jou telling Snake that jou can put people away in different countries."

"Yeeeah…man…guess I kinda said too much." Brandon says scratching his neck looking around the room. Odeo reaches into the drawer and pulls out a stack of bills, fanning them in his hand.

Brandon is looking guiltily down at his shoes. "Yeah, well man, see that's the part of my job I don't like to…" Brandon looks up, distracted by constant movement in his side vision, he stares questionably at Odeo, seeing the waving bills. "Is this what I think it is?" Brandon asks.

"Most likely."

"Maaan…you don't even know all the de…" Odeo slams the stack of cash on top of the desk.

"We know enough." Odeo says then takes a deep breath. "I need this favor bad,maaan.

Yo, if he gets locked up, I continue running this joint, pay myself more and do more for my family, man. Plus, jou're gonna need somebody to keep jour car in tack whenever jou even think sum'ting may feel like it's wrong with it. No? All jour car problems will be fixed free, on me, even the routine maintenance—oil changes, tires rotated. Hell, even if jou go to my manacross the way to get your gas tank filled, I'll see to it that'll be free for jou too." Brandon glances back and forth from Odeo to the money.

CHAPTER 50

Snake and Sli glare as they relentlessly point their guns at each other's faces. Haddie is holding the gun downward in her hand. "I cannot believe yall doing this to each other. Acting like some savage beasts raised yall asses. I know damn well I taught yall better."

"Don't you mean she's doing this to me, Ma? She tried to kill my daughter, your only granddaughter. And she may have already succeeded in killing my son since nobody heard from him." Snake says.

"Oooh nigga palease. Yo li' thieving ass kids need to be punished by somebody since you won't do it. First, she stole my diamond earrings. Now she steals my money and other stuff of mine. I had to show her she won't be stealing nothing else from me. And I know *your son* is in on it too, or at least he knows something, 'cause I'm sure you do remember many of our secrets that we swore *never* to tell nobody." Sli remindshim.

"Aw come on, she was a little girl when she took those earrings. She didn't know no better and at least you could've gotten 'em back but you wanted the money instead. But you know damn well she aint took shit else from you since." Snake says.

"And how would you know? As a matter of fact, you never even paid me my fifteen hunerd for those earrings either." Sli cocks her gun. "Since you sound so mighty damned knowing maybe it was *you*!"

Haddie's shoulders drop as her head tilts to one side. "Sli… please tell me you didn't do nothing to Tyler."

Sli rolls her eyes then looks intensely at Haddie. "No." "Then where is he?" Haddie asks.

"How am I supposed to know? He aint my son." "That's right, Sli. Yo' son dead." Snake says coldly. Sli cuts her eyes at Snake.

"Oh, come on now!" Haddie says, flinging her arms, hoping to squelch the tension. "That's what all this about? Material crap, Sli?"

Nicky and several other people duck in different directions. "Watch out there now with that gun Mama! I'm not ready to die!" Nicky says.

Streng looks frustrated, widening his eyes at Felanie. "And yo' dumb ass gave her yo' piece."

"And this coming from a nigga with a decimated cerebral cortex." Felanie retorts. Nicky grins after looking around and having a second thought. You know this *is* the perfect spot to get shot though. Probably could get a good lick out that shit too." Nicky straightens her posture as if preparing for a bullet to hit her. "Girrrlfriend a'ight I'm ready! You can accidently shoot me now."

Sli rolls her eyes, lowers her gun, then looks Haddie in the eyes. "Oh, Mama give me a break. You beat me down over the twenty dollars I took out yo' purse 'cause I wanted to go on a school field trip that you wouldn't sign for and I had to have someone else sign for. So, I could only imagine you woulda done me worse had it been ten thousand."

"Ten thousand dollars!" Haddie yells, placing her hands on her hips. "You had ten thousand dollars and you barely paying me yo' three hundred dollars rent every month." Haddie says, getting in Sli' face as she continues flinging her armsaround.

Snake lowers his gun. "Ha! Now who's a thief." Hemocks.

Sli turns to Snake. "Yeah, well guess what thief was about to be taking her lil' ass a dirt nap."

Snake points his gun at Sli. "And like I said that shit won't be happenin' no mo'." Sli points her gun at Snake.

Haddie stomps her feet. "Wait one got damn minute! Don't yall remember how yall used to play everything together. Snake, you enjoyed helping your twin dress her dolls. Yall did everything and went everywhere together. Don't yall remember that? What happened? Yall loved each other so much and now nobody would even know yall even related much less twins from the same egg." Haddie's voice starts cracking as she holds back tears. She walks closer to Sli. "Sli, what brother you know will spend as much time with they sister as Snake did with you? Most brothers enjoy torturing sisters." Haddie smiles with tears lingering in hereyes.

Haddie walks closer to Snake. "And Snake, Remember, how you and Sli would play with your green plastic army figurines…pretending like yall were on the war field against each other. Yall would say silly stuff that made no sense." Haddie looks back and forth at Sli and Snake. "Sli said stuff like 'Boy you better give me back my country or I'll burn down all yo' flowers and trees and take away all yo' oxygen.'" Haddie laughs as tears roll down her cheeks. "Because after you learned in your science class that plants, or is it trees? Well, whichever one it is that give off oxygen, you thought people would easily die if they were destroyed." Haddie giggles.

Haddie looks at Snake again. "And Snake don't you remember how you was always fighting some boy, and some girls too, who would mess with your sister. You were always her protector. Yall made me so proud to be yall Mama." More rears fall from Haddie's eyes. She steps back to wave her arms around. "And now look at yall dumb asses out here actin' like another unnecessary American war."

Sli and Snake's faces soften. They both slowly lower their guns. But then Snake has a flashback of Tawny's swollen face. "Naw! Fuck that, Ma! You saw my baby's swollen face? She got a concussion 'cause Sli beat her with a bag of bricks! And aint no telling what other damages done. And for all I know she may have succeeded in killing my son."

Snake turns and points his gun toward Felanie and Streng. "And you mufukas helped her!

Where's my muthafukin son!" Streng and Felanie cower.

Diana jumps up from her seat and rushes to stand near Snake, Haddie and Sli. "Yep! I bet they know somethin' 'cause when I went downstairs to tell her about Bryk being rushed here she had Tawny sitting in a chair and I could hear her begging for water."

Snake waves his arms around. "I can't believe you could do something so heartless to yo own flesh and blood, man! This shit got me ALL fucked up in the head!" He points the gun at Sli. "It's sad it's come to this, but you started it and now I need to finish this shit." Snake says with clenched jaws. Snake fights back tears as he stumbles and falls against the wall. He stands straight again. His face contorts with anger and his arms and body fiercely tremble as he raises his gun and points it firmly at Sli again. Sli quickly points her gun at Snake.

"Wait! What are yall doing? Stop it!" Diana screams. "Put the guns down! Now!" Haddie commands.

Snake and Sli stare at each other as they slowly lower their guns. Haddie's mouth drops open and eyes widen as she looks with terror then disdain at Sli then at Snake and back at Sli again. "Now I know damn well you didn't hurt my grand baby like that! Your own niece, Sli?"

"Mama whatchu think I've been sayin' all this time? She didn't just hurt her she tried to kill my baby. She actually put her in a casket and drove around to find a spot to bury her in. We would've never known what the hell happened if the cops hadn't pulled her over! They the ones got my baby out the casket." Snake says.

Diana puts her hands over her mouth. "Oh my God, Sli you wanted to kill your only niece? You have sincerely gone crazy. Are you on crack or something?"

Sli looks at Diana. "You need to get the fuck out my face. You know I asked you about my shit that got stolen." Sli points the gun at Diana. "You said you didn't do it but for all I know you could've been the ringleader. Scheming with that li' thieving bitch." Sli face grimaces in anger. "My son is dead and all yall wanna talk about is a thief as if what she did is acceptable!

This just shows yall don't care shit about me!" Tears fall from Sli's eyes.

A tear falls from Snake's eye, as he grasps the gun tighter. Haddie looks puzzled and broken hearted at Sli and Snake. She then throws both arms in the air and grunts in frustration. "What is really going on right now? Yall don't wanna hurt each other like this. It's apparent we are all hurting. Just put the guns down so we can all talk about it." Sli and Snake slowly lower their guns.

Snake gets another flashback of Tawny. "No! No! Hell Naw! My baby could've died from that beating!" With rage in his eyes, he points the gun at Sli again, spreads his legs, rocking his tense body from side to side. "Where's my son, Sli!" Sli stands in the same position toward Snake.

"I'm sure there's more that's been done. Yall just not telling it." Snake says.

"All you need to know is that your precious little girl stole my shit and wouldn't give it back, so I handled it. I don't know nothing about your son. Apparently, you don't keep up with neither of them enough to know nothing yourself. ...Besides you already know how we do it. What you thought things would be done differently because we *family*? Naw, fuck that bro." Sli says.

Haddie flings her arms around again, stomping as she paces back and forth. "God damn it! Now I done already told yall...Put the fucking guns down! I raised yall better than this! Now you got me questioning where the fuck *did* I go wrong? I know I was a bit rough on yall sometimes but got damn it...I thought I still instilled in yall's brain that blood is always thicker than mud."

Sli lets out a long and loud sigh. "Blood is thicker than mud! Ha! Really, Mama." She drops her arms then looks at Haddie. "See Ma that's...your...fucking...problem! You don't really believe that bullshit you're saying. How many times we've had parties at the house and some muthufuckin body stole something?"

"You watch yo mouth!" Haddie says between clenched teeth.

Sli continues speaking as if her mother said nothing. "If blood is so much thicker than mud, why haven't you invited them back to the house? But that little bitch can steal from me, and I can't stop her from coming to our house because that's your sweet little grandbaby. Sooo I did what I had to do to stop her."

"Now I'm gonna do what the fuck I gotta do!" Snake says cocking his gun.

Sli quickly raises her gun toward Snake and cocks it. "Well now, that makes both of us, muthafuka!"

"I'm not gon' say it no mo'! Yall put them muthafukin guns down!" Haddie demands.

Haddie steps in between them, extends her arms to push them both backward. "This shit is gone end right now!" Haddie's gun goes off.

Sli and Snake shoot at one another. Snake's bullet strikes Sli. Sli falls down.

The bullet from Sli's gun hits Haddie in the neck. The emergency room's automatic glass door shatters. Haddie falls to the floor.

"MA!" Diana screams as she falls to her knees to hold Haddie in her arms. "MAMA!" Snake yells as he scrambles toward Haddie.

Sli lies on the ground staring at everyone.

CHAPTER 51

Outside the emergency room the sound of shattering glass causes officers to duck and draw their guns toward the emergency room doors. An officer speaks into a megaphone. "It's over! You all need to come the fuck out now with your hands up…unless your dumb asses are already dead!"

The officer gestures to another officer. "Send that kid over here." Tyler walks over to the officer. The Officer whispers in Tyler's ear then holds the megaphone in front of Tyler's mouth.

"Daddy! Please come out! I'm scared and wanna go home!"

Hearing Tyler's voice Snake looks with mixed emotions toward the automatic doors.

Relieved to hear his son's voice he slowly sits up. When he looks and notices Haddie still has not moved as Diana holds her in her arms wailing, he slides toward them.

Sli is in a state of shock as she lies on the floor bleeding. She stares at Haddie's limp body lying beside her. Sli manages to sit up. But when she looks around and notices the massive amount of blood surrounding her, she passes out. Doctors and nurses run toward them.

"Sliiii!" Nicky lets out a high-pitched squeal. "Wake yo' ass up! This the wrong time to be passin' the fuck out! Bitch you bet not die on me!" Nicky grabs her head with her hands. "I swear fo God you bet not die. I need my hair done…Shit!" Nicky yells.

Streng and Felanie walk outside with their hands up. Snake is behind them with his one good arm up. Cops have guns pointed at them. "Stop right there and lie down on the ground!" An officer commands through the megaphone.

Officers swarm toward Snake, Streng and Felanie to handcuff them. Jingling bells are heard approaching followed by Cooper's voice:

Fresh off the freight, so you know it's great!
My name is Cooper, but you can call me Coop.
Accessories: from bangles, bags to boots.
Got toys for yo' kids that can spin, sang, or shoot.
Wanna eat?
Got those sour, sugary, and salty treats.
Need something at home?
Check out my cutlery, candles, brushes and combs.
If you need it, and I don't got it, just let it be known.
I'll cop it when I can. I SWEAR the wait won't be long.
Be back here in a flash; sangin' this same ole song.

CHAPTER 52

Diana, Tawny, Tyler and Ted are at Haddie's gravesite with roses. They each set a rose on the grass. Diana sobs as she hugs Haddie's tombstone. Tyler, Tawny and Ted console her.

They then walk over to place flowers on Bryk's gravesite, only a few feet away. They hold each other and cry.

CHAPTER 53

Brandon walks into a private room where Snake is already seated. Brandon removes his suit jacket, places it on the back of his chair, then reaches into his brief case on the floor beside him, to get papers. He glances over documents. "Okay, so we have witnesses claiming you have a daughter who is known to act out. It says here, 'theft, disturbance of the peace'…"

"What! Man, that's a ball faced lie. That was damn near ten years ago when she borrowed a pair of earrings from her auntie. But my sister could've got her shit back though if she wasn't so damned stubborn. That was the only time…"

"Okay well that's not what the police reports are saying."

"Police reports? The fuck you mean? My daughter aint no damn criminal! My sister tried to *kill her*, maaan. Put her in a coffin and was about to bury her. Nobody thinks that's enough evidence to fucking put her ass away for life?" Snake's voice changes mockingly into a high-pitched white man's voice. "I mean after all it is considered attempted murder by most judiciary standards." He gets serious again and speaks in his natural tone but raises his voice. "Okay…so, let's just say my daughter did steal. That's nothing compared to her own aunt trying to kill her. Not to mention she actually succeeded in killing our mother. So yeah, murder *should* account for something in this equation. Right?" Snake puts his elbows on the table, placing his head between his hands.

Brandon sighs. "Okay…you calm for good now? If you keep getting irate and giving these long ass sermons, we won't get anything accomplished…Speaking of getting nothing accomplished I went to see yo' baby mama. You said she was supposed to give me $5,000 and all she gave me was four. Now I don't know what type of games yall playin'…

"Wait…Jessica didn't give you all the money?" Brandon raises his eyebrows and tilts his head.

"Okay…Okay. I'll get you the rest of yo' money, man." Snake assures him.

Brandon continues. "Now as I was saying her background check shows that she has criminal records for…" Snake jerks his head to look up at Brandon.

"When you say *her* you talkin' 'bout my sister right?"

"Nooo, Snake I'm still talking about your daughter…Let's see…it says here breaking and entering, trespassing."

Snake jumps up, knocking his chair over. "Wait…one…got…damn…minute! This bet not be what I think it is!" Snake slams his fist on the table. "Got damn it! Who the fuck is paying you!"

"You know what…" Brandon says, gathering his papers, then stuffing them into his briefcase.

Snake's entire body is shaking with rage. "My sister got to you, didn't she? How much you take from her?"

Brandon ignores Snake's questions as he continues packing his things away.

Snake picks his chair up and sits back down. "You guilty as fuck the reason you can't answer my questions! All I need is for you to help me put her far away like you do for all those other folks you told me about."

Brandon grinding his teeth, points his finger harshly into Snake's face. "You need to shut yo' damned mouth…before both of us get locked up, somewhere for life." Brandon stands up, grabs his suit jacket from the back of the chair and puts it on. He leans on the table, looking Snake in the eyes. "And just so you know I've never even met your sister. So, no, I could not have taken anything from her because she didn't offer me anything. Now on that note let's do this some other time, when you're more levelheaded and less accusatory." Brandon walks toward the door, then turns to look back at Snake. "Call me when you think you're ready. Guard!"

CHAPTER 54

Nicky is sitting at the table, eating a sandwich and sipping her drink. A McDonald's paper bag sits near her elbow. The security officer walks in with Sli, who is limping with a cane. She sits down across from Nicky.

"Thanks for looking out, Marcus!" Nicky says, chewing.

"Whatever, dude!" This bet not come back to bite me in the ass… or else…" Marcus says, sticking up his middle finger, he is about to shut the door.

Nicky takes a quick bite of her sandwich, then looks up at Marcus with a sly grin. "Hey Marcus…Speaking of biting in the ass…" She stands up, bends over with her ass facing Marcus and twerks, while chewing just as fast as her ass in jiggling.

Marcus's face contorts with disgust before closing the door.

Nicky offers Sli a sandwich. Sli bites into it. "Yuck! I hate Micky D's, but anything is better than this shit in here." Sli says, holding up her sandwich. "Thanks though…Look at you! Looking all dignified in yo' court clerk uniform." Sli says grinning at Nicky.

"Bitch please! I hate this ugly ass jacket. I was thinking about adding some bling to it. But that'll give them a legitimate reason to fire my Black ass fasho. And if me and Marcus get caught making this visit happen during my work hours, we gone both be out the door." Nicky balls up the wrapper her sandwich was in and tosses it into the paper bag next to her as she continues talking. "Okay, so, I was at the shop letting Tyana do my hair, and I heard Adisa telling her customer that she's looking for somebody to rent out yo' booth. Girrrlfriend! We gotta hurry up and getcho ass outta here so…"

"Bitch…focus! What did yo lawyer dude friend say?"

"Brandon? Oh yeah, I told him aboutchu but he not gon' talk to me like that about yo' case. You need to get him in here so you can talk to him first. Tell him you want me to help you out with this. Plus, once he puts a face to yo' name, he can see what he's working with."

Nicky stands to twerk again, then drops it like it's hot. "Girrrlfriend! I had to use some of my surgery money to buy me a new car." She throws one leg on the table, continuing to gyrate. "But I'm getting closer to the amount I need again, so I'll be a full-fledged woman hopefully reeeal soon this time for real, bitch." She grabs ahold of the back of Sli's chair, dancing seductively. "I gotta get up and celebrate er'time I think about that shit. I don't care where I'm at...unless I'm in the courtroom." She stands next to Sli. "Then I gotta do it like this." Nicky jiggles her body softly, almost unnoticeably.

Sli rolls her eyes. "Damn Nicky! Yo' ass making me nervous. I got to get the fuck outta here as soon as possible and you shakin' yo' ass like this a game or some shit. Can you just tell him to come see me please?"

Nicky is dancing her way back to her chair. "Okay. But *you* better wake the fuck up! The real game is all about that pussy." She puts her foot on the seat, gyrating, then finally plops down, sitting in her seat, sounding winded. "You ever heard that sayin'? I don't know what the problem is, but the answer is usually pussy?" Nicky jerks her neck, staring with wide eyes at Sli.

Sli takes a deep breath then lets it out. "Can you at least have him come talk to me tomorrow?"

Nicky stretches out her tongue, touching her nose then quickly jiggling it around. "Whatchu think?" Nicky asks looks at Sli questionably.

Sli rolls her eyes, then rubs her forehead. She stands up, grabs her cane and stares at Nicky exasperated. She takes a step, then winces in pain, grabbing her thigh. "I think that mufuka gon' have to pay for putting a hurting on me like this. I'm just glad he didn't hit me in my arm or hands like I got his ass 'cause that woulda fucked with my money maker. Anyway, Nicky please make it happen. You got me scared as hell that I'm gonna be stuck in here cause yo' ass is playin' too much. Security!" Sli yells

"Bitch, I gotchu! I don't like the way that bitch did my hair anyway so yo' ass gots to get the fuck outta here." Nicky loudly slurps the last of her drink before standing and grabbing her belongings. "Okay I'm about to go to his office and talk to him as soon as my lunch is over…in a few minutes." Nicky assures Sli Marcus opens the door. Sli walks out, heading toward the direction of her cell, as Marcus walks behind her.

Nicky struts next to Marcus before going ahead of him to jiggle her ass. "You think you can afford or handle all of this occiferrr?"

Marcus turns his lips up, as if unphased. "Nigga please! I wasn't on that shit when we played basketball at Crane together, when you kept pulling this same shit then. Aint nothin' changed, Nicholas. I still aint into dicks. I got my own." Marcus grabs his crouch. "Big and strong and the only one I need. So just keep walkin' yo dizzy ass on and lose all that jiggling bullshit."

Nicky turns around to face him as she walks backward. "Shiiiit! I done heard it all before, big man. Let a nigga get horny enough. All that shit talk goes in hiding, especially behind closed doors."

"Yeah, you are absolutely right about that one. I'll be behind closed doors, a'ight…Behind that bolted metal door, dead in a morgue, 'cause that's the only way that shit's gonna happen."

CHAPTER 55

Nicky knocks on Brandon's office door. "Enter!" Brandon yells. She walks in. Brandon stares blankly at her.

"Hey boo!" Nicky says with excitement.

Brandon leans back in his chair. "Now what do you want?"

"Wait." Nicky says as she closes the door and rushes to sit down. "Just hear me out before you get all irritated again. I have a best friend who was locked up for something she had no control of 'cause she was just protecting what's hers. Right?

"Come on now, Nicky. That's the same shit every criminal claims. That, and they didn't do it." Brandon makes air quotes. "I need you to speed this along I have an appointment coming in a few minutes."

"Okay, okay…so she's been locked up for attempted murder or manslaughter, or something like that, and some other shit, and she needs you to help her to get free. Plus…make sure her twin brother gets the maximum and sent some faraway place, so he'll never make his way back to anywhere in Amerrreka." Nicky says with a Hispanic accent.

Brandon looks puzzled at Nicky, as he adjusts his body, and begins fidgeting with an ink pen.

"Well damn! I've heard of sibling rivalry but that's fucked up to want your own brother put away. And to think twins are usually best friends."

"I'm sure it'll all make sense once you get the full story from her. But you need to go see her so she can tell you everything."

Brandon slowly shakes his head "I can't make any promises.".

Nicky stands, strutting toward Brandon, she stops beside him and turns his chair so he's facing her. Looking down at him she stands between his legs. "So exactly what will it take to get you to promise me you'll at least go talk to her and try to help her?" Nicky asks in her sexiest tone.

Brandon looks Nicky up and down. His eyes widen when Nicky quickly drops down on her knees and begins unfastening Brandon's belt and unzipping his pants. She places his penis in her mouth. Brandon's Adam's apple protrudes as he lays his head back, revealing the whites of eyes as his eyelids semi close.

Nicky stops to look up at him. Brandon looks down at Nicky with one eye open. "Why am I doing this Brandon?" Nicky asks.

"What are you talking about?"

Nicky raises her eyebrows and purses her lips.

Brandon throws his hands up. "Okaaay…whatchu want me to say? Yo' girl in jail and…You know what…never mind." Brandon begins fastening his clothes.

There's a knock at the door. Brandon quickly stands, scrambling faster to make himself presentable. Nicky remains on her knees, unfazed.

"One minute!" Brandon yells toward the door, then quickly sits down to look Nicky in the face to whisper. "The fuck is you doing? Get yo ass up!"

"You still aint promised nuthin' though." Nicky reminds him.

He throws his arms in the air then lets them drop to rest on his seat. "Okay, okay. I promise." Brandon assures, as he grips the seat with intensity.

The door swings open. Tyler and Tawny walks in. Nicky quickly looks around on the floor as if looking for a lost item. As Diana walks in behind them, Nicky stands up slowly, staring with envy.

"Oh, I'm sorry I thought I heard someone say come in." Diana says embarrassed.

Nicky gets a sly grin on her face. She looks at Brandon, who is still staring mesmerized by Diana's beauty. "It's okay sweetheart. Come on in. Brandon and I were just finishing up some important business." Nicky looks at Brandon, expecting him to agree but he doesn't respond, as he continues staring at Diana.

Still kneeling near the side of Brandon's desk, Nicky finally stands. She leans over, placing both of her hands atop of it. "Weren't we Brandon?"

"Oh…Yeah, yeah." Brandon says as he stands up. "At least two of you can get comfortable while I go grab another chair." Brandon says, stealing glances at Diana, until he's finally outside of his office. Nicky leaves with him.

Brandon grabs a chair from the lobby's waiting area. Nicky walks alongside him, attempting to whisper. "Don't you dare try to play me, Brandon…I mean my friend. And don't be losing focus over that bitch in there 'cause I know exactly who she is and why she's here. I see how she got you in there gawking. So, you can stop all that right now." Her tone switches from angry to flirtatious. "'Cause I'm the only one who needs to help you with that, sweetheart." Nicky exaggeratedly swings her hips as she struts away. Brandon rolls his eyes, grabs a chair and returns to hisoffice.

Using his foot to shut the door, he holds the chair in his hands as he speaks. "Hello again everyone! Did you miss me?"

They all look at each other, smiling awkwardly. Brandon chuckles. "Probably not.

Anyway…I'm Brandon Barnes." Brandon sets the chair down in front of his desk, then extends his arm to shake Diana's hand. And *you* must be Ms. Diana Maldive. The handshake lingers longer than normal.

"And who are these beautiful young people that I have the pleasure of meeting?"

"My twin niece and nephew Tawny and Tyler." Brandon shakes the twin's hands.

"I am pleased to meet all of you." Brandon says, staring directly at Diana. He directs his attention at Tyler. "Young man you shake like you can throw a mean football. You on the football team at school?" Brandon asks as he sits at his desk, pecking on the keyboard.

Tyler shakes his head. "Naw."

"Well then you gots to be basketball player?" "Naw, man I don't play no sports."

Brandon looks shocked. "Well maybe you should think about it. You'll probably tear something up on any of those fields."

Brandon takes a deep breath. "Now…what can I do for you Ms. Maldive, or can I call you Diana?"

"Diana's fine. My brother, their dad, Snake's been locked up for something he shouldn't be, and he said that I should come see you because you would know what to do to get him out."

Brandon looks taken aback at the mention of Snake's name. "Okay. Start from the beginning and tell me everything, at least as much as you know."

Diana tells her whole version of the events as Brandon writes notes on a yellow legal pad.

Her voice begins cracking when she gets to the part about her mom getting killed by Sli. She stops talking when tears roll down her eyes. Brandon passes her a tissue.

Tawny looks at Tyler. "You heard him say tell him everything." Tawny says. Diana looks with confusion from Tawny to Tyler.

"What's going on yall?" Diana asks blowing her nose.

Tyler looks down at the floor and responds solemnly. "I'm the one took auntie Sli stuff." "What are you saying?" Diana asks, wiping her nose with the tissue.

"I snuck in auntie Sli's apartment one day when everybody had left the building and took her stuff. I only wanted some fireworks but tried on her jewelry and liked it, so I decided to borrow that too. Then I kept looking around and found her money. I had it all in my bag but then Bryk found it and took it from me."

"Who is Bryk?" Brandon asks as he wipes his face with the palm of his hand, anticipating the case being more complicated than he expected.

Tears roll down Tyler's eyes. Brandon passes him a tissue.

"Bryk is my nephew. He's my sister's son. My sister and Snake are twins." Diana says.

Everyone is silent a few seconds when Diana stands up harshly, holding her hand on her forehead she paces behind her chair. She stops pacing then glares at Tyler. "You do realize your sister could've been killed because of you! And Mama..." Holding back tears, Diana runs out of the office.

Brandon snatches a few tissues from the Kleenex box then places the box into Tawny's hands as he runs out the office to catch up with Diana.

Tyler folds his arms, resting his elbows on the desk, he places his forehead on his arms, and sobs. "I'm sorry, yall...I'm so sorry...I'm sorry, Bryk...I'm sooo sorry, Grandmaaa..."

Tawny consoles him.

CHAPTER 56

Sli is giving details of what led to her incarceration. Brandon is listening and taking notes. He puts his pen down. "Before we go any further let's get the financing out the way. How are you paying me?"

"Let me write down his information."

Sli picks up Brandon's legal pad and tears a blank sheet off and writes on it. "This my baby daddy. His name is Bruno. I already told him you were coming to get $5,000 so he'll have it for you." Once Sli hands Brandon the paper he slips it into his shirt pocket.

"Okay. So, what makes you so sure your niece stole your stuff?" Brandon asks.

Sli leans back in her chair. "Maaan, come on…were you not listening to nothing I just said? Cause she did that shit before. I know it was her. Only a dumb bi…"

"So, what if we have witnesses who say your son Bryk, is actually the one who stole your things? Let's see…" Brandon scrambles through papers and picks one.

Sli looks angrily at Brandon. "Who the fuck toldchu that lie?"

"It's all right here. The coroner's report says: Cause of death; burn shock caused by hypovolemia…'

Sli is slowly shaking her head then stands up. Brandon stares at her a few seconds as he continues reading without looking at the paper. "'… due to damaged blood vessels and sepsis.'"

Sli backs up against the wall, shaking her head faster, trying to process it. Brandon looks at the paper. "'Approximately eighty percent along the back and neck, consists of skin lacerations caused by fireworks explosion.' Brandon puts the paper away. "Now, I understand you were missing fireworks, correct?"

Sli screams, sliding down the wall crying uncontrollably. "Noooooo! My baby wouldn't do nothing like that to me!"

Brandon stares at Sli a few seconds then walks to the door, knocks and beckons through the window for the guard. Two guards walk in to pick Sli up from the floor. Brandon gathers his things then puts on his suit jacket. Sli is softly mumbling and sobbing. "I know this is a bit much to take in," Brandon says. "I'll come back another day to finish our discussion." He's about to walk out but stops and turns to look back. "You may want to consider getting professional counseling to help you deal with all of this." Brandon walks away as Sli's wailing fades behind him.

CHAPTER 57

Rock and his wife walk into the Golden Nugget restaurant. "Table for two please," Rock tells the hostess.

"It's about a half hour wait," the hostess tells him. Rock nods and gives his name so that the hostess could write it down. He points to an empty seat on the end of the bench. His wife sits while he stands next to her.

"Yooo, da fuck jou mean it aint lookin' gud, homes?" Odeo asks, leaning forward and patting the envelope setting on the table. "Dis makes five fuckin' G's. *Lookin' gud* aint an option, man. Look…I'm just as hard workin' for mine as…"

Brandon puts of forkful of food into his mouth then drops the fork onto his almost empty plate, causing a loud clinging sound.

Rock, who is conversing with his wife, is startled by the cling, which makes him look in the direction of where Odeo and Brandon are sitting. "There go that Hispanic nigga, at my job I be telling you about. I'll be back baby," Rock says, then heads toward Odeo and Brandon.

Brandon leans forward, about to check Odeo, when Rock appears. "What's up O! Didn't expect to run into you in a place like this," Rock says grinning.

"A nigga like me gotta eat too, homes." Odeo retorts.

"Yeah, but they don't specialize in taco cuisines and orange rice platters here though, bro. '"Cause I know you probably thought this was like Taco Bell and shit." Rocks says, nodding with asmirk.

Odeo squints at Rock. Rock looks at Brandon. "Oh…hey dude. I've seen you at the shop."

"Yeah…brought my ride in," Brandon responds.

"So, you got er'thang you need? Yo' Lexus running smooth now?" Rock asks. "Yeah, everything all good now. Thanks." Brandon says, rubbing his hands together. "Rock. Table for two." The Hostess yells.

Rock looks toward the hostess and sees his wife standing up. He puts his finger up to show her he'll be joining her, then looks back at Odeo and Brandon. "A'ight. Cool. Cool." Rock says nodding. "Well, that's me they just called." Rock looks down at the envelope. Brandon notices, snatches the envelope and puts it in his jacket pocket.

"A'ight. Yall stay cool." Rock says before walking away.

Brandon and Odeo remain quiet until Rock is out of ear shot. "Listen! There's a lot more involved with this case that you'll never know about. But I'm not going to discuss that part with you right now, maybe even never," Brandon says, then rapidly pokes his jacket. "But what I will say is these little pieces of pennies you think I should be worshipping you over has to be split into several more quarter pieces in order to properly pay everybody involved." Brandon grinds his teeth and squints his eyes. "So, since that still leaves me shit for pay, I suggest, if you want some guarantees, you up the ante on more of those got damn G'S you worshipping."

They stare at one another as Odeo sucks his teeth and Brandon takes a sip from his cup.

CHAPTER 58

Brandon sets his cup down. "Okay…so…just for the record this is not an official date…yet. Reason being we're discussing business as attorney and client. Just so you know, when we're officially dating there will be no more business to discuss because the case will be closed, unless *you* would like to discuss something else. So, now that I've gotten that I've gotten that out the way, we'll get back to business." Brandon takes another drink. "If you could possibly get one more witness, preferably an adult, to testify that they saw Bryk with Sli's stolen possessions it would make the case against her stronger."

Diana shakes her head. "If someone does know they're not telling it."

"I, honest to God, don't want to pit the twins against each other. They've already experienced enough madness in one lifetime. I wouldn't want Tawny to have to testify against her brother and I damn sure don't want Tyler incriminating himself," Brandon assures Diana.

"Right…Tell me about it." Diana says as she takes a drink from her cup, smiling at Brandon as she puts it back down.

Brandon smiles back. "Okay…now that we've gotten business out the way let's talk about us…" Brandon says as he takes each of Diana's hands.

Diana blushes flirtatiously. "Well, one thing I must confess, this my first time eating at Priscilla's Soul Food Restaurant."

Brandon raises his eyebrows. "Well, is it now? Now we'll have to see what other things we need to make our firsts."

Diana's grin spreads wider as she releases a soft chuckle and gently squirms in her seat.

Instrumental music plays softly as they continue conversing until the restaurant closes.

CHAPTER 59

"Man, I saw that nigga, O' and that bald-headed customer you so cool wit' eating together at the restaurant the other day. Dude snatched a envelope after he saw me looking at it…I tolchu not to hire that mufuka, Odeo. Even his *name* sound dumb as fuck. Butchu just wouldn't listen to me talkin' 'bout how good he is fixing cars and shit." Rock says, flinging his hands and arms to emphasize his point. "I knew that nigga was full of shit when I first smelled his funky ass. I always figured it was somethin' up with him. I know *yo'* name Snake but that muthufuka the real snake," Rock says.

Snake raises his eyebrows, rubbing his beard, listening and staring in a daydream. "Yeeeah, that was Brandon. And here I was thinking my sister got a hold of him but now I see it's O' fake ass. His ass still mad 'cause I didn't give him that advance he wanted." Snake snaps out of his daydream and faces Rock. "Man, the real reason I hired his ass is 'cause yo' ass been lacking on the job…"

"Lacking? Man, you crazy as hell…I may have had to take off a few times but when I'm actually there I aint never lacking on shit."

"And in those few days I lost too much fucking money, nigga…" Snake snaps. "Maaan…" Rock gives him the forget you wave. "Anyway, the first time I saw them together was when I was leaving to go get me some lunch and Brandon walked in. He was gone when I got back, and I saw O' working on his car so apparently he had him to hook him up quick."

Snake rubs his forehead then puts pressure on both eyelids with his thumb and index fingers. "Yeeeah…the parts did come in the day before I got locked up. I just didn't get a chance…"

"Well, I don't know what that was about, but I bet O' making deals behind yo' back.

Probably giving that discounts and shit," Rock interrupts. "Or worse giving him free shit. Robbing you more than you claim I did. Man, you need to check that nigga.".

"You mean *you* need to be checking that nigga for me. I can't do nothing in here." Snake reminds him.

Rock humps his shoulders. "Well, you know man there's only so much I can do 'cause he done changed the locks on the doors. So, he opens and closes when he wants. And now he even got some of his boys working on cars. One of them fools even be acting like he O's damned bodyguard. I'm telling you dude it's crazy." Rock shakes his head

A security officer walks to the middle of the room. "Visitation is over! Cell mates line up along the orange wall to my left and wait until the door opens! Visitors you will remain seated until all cell mates have exited the visitation area!"

"Well, keep me posted, man and thanks for lookin' out," Snake says, standing.

"A'ight man…I'll see what I can do." Rock assures him, standing so they can lock hands, hug and give each other a pat on the back before departing.

A security officer sees Rock standing. "Hey you! Sit down!"

Rock shakes his head and sits back down. "Yeah, Man you gon' have to hurry up and get the fuck outta here 'cause this some bullshit."

CHAPTER 60

Nicky and Brandon are on their lunch breaks, sitting in the front seat of Brandon's car talking. Once they're done eating, Nicky climbs into the back seat. Brandon exits the driver's side door to slip into the back seat next to Nicky.

The volume on the radio is low but the lyrics are clear:

> *These are the tales. The freaky tales*
> *These are the tales that I tell so well*
> *These are the tales. The freaky tales*
> *These are the tales that I tell so well*
> *I met this girl her name is Joan*
> *She loved the way I rock on the microphone*
> *When I met Joan I took her home*
> *She was just like a doggie all on my bone*
> *I met another girl her name was Ann*
> *All she wanted was to freak with a man*
> *When I met Ann I shook her hand*
> *We ended up freakin' by a garbage can…*

The song "Freaky Tales" by Too Short continues as Nicky covers her head it bobs up and down between Brandon's legs. Brandon breathes heavily; his eyes roll to the back of his head, as his neck extends back. He opens his eyes and begins tapping on Nicky's shoulder rapidly, barely able to get his words out. "Stop! Stop! Stop moving! Somebody's getting in the car next to us.

Aw, shit! I'm on edge!"

Nicky ignores Brandon and continues working on him. Brandon tenses up and yells out in ecstasy.

****

An hour later, Brandon is looking fatigued when he visits Snake. They sit across from each other at a desk in a private room. Snake holds up his hands. "Before we get started, did Jessica pay you the rest of the money?"

"Yeah…" Brandon sighs, raises his eyebrows and hesitates before continuing to speak. "And I tried hard as hell to find more evidence in your defense. Unfortunately, things aint looking any better for you." He leans forward, resting his elbows on the table. "But what I did find out is that it was Tyler who stole from Sli. But somehow Bryk ended up stealing from Tyler the stuff Tyler stole from Sli, which is how Bryk ended up setting himself on fire at the park."

Snake looks at him stunned. "Wait…So what you're telling me is that my son was the one who stole from my sister?" Snake shakes his head vigorously. "Naaaw… maaan…I don't believe that shit."

"Well, you can just ask him yourself the next time you talk to him or when he comes to see you."

"Naw I don't want him seeing me in here like this. I'll call him today to see what's really going on."

Brandon pulls papers from his bag, staring extra-long at one. "In the meantime, I got new information that could really do damage to your case…" Brandon slides the paper across the table so Snake could look at it. Brandon waits a few minutes to give him time to read it.

"So, who is Grenely Brown?" Brandon asks, breaking the silence.

Snake's forehead wrinkles. "He was a mutual friend of the family, who lived down the block from our house. He was like the handy man at our building. If something needed fix…"

"You said he *was*, as in past tense. What happened?" Brandon interrupts. Snake hesitates. "I don't know…Nobody's seen him in a while…"

"Well maybe I can refreshen your memory for you. There are witnesses saying they suspected something was wrong when he didn't show up at your mom's house on the fourth of July for her backyard barbecue. The first issue here is his mom confirmed that he was expected to travel back home with a group in a carpool to visit her for the holiday. But the second biggest problem is he never showed up at his mom's. Nor was he seen anywhere down south during the time he was expected to be there. But the third crucial issue here is several witnesses, are in agreement, that *you* murdered Grenely."

Snake snaps up from his seat harshly. "That's a mufuckin lie! Dude whose side you really on! I know aint nobody, but Sli and her flunkies, told you that bullshit! What other lies did she tell you?"

Brandon, with tight lips, stare up at Snake then squeezes his eyes with his thumb and index finger and exhales. "Look man, these outbursts aint helping you. And now that you're the major suspect in Grenely's disappearance this is just another setback in your case. So, if you don't get witnesses or proof that you're innocent in all of these accusations against you…Well you already know the deal"

Snake leans forward, with his palms on the table, whispering between tight lips. "But aint you the one who told me you can convict anyone based on fake shit?"

"Hey man I don't know what you're talking about. So as of right now you need to start spilling it all if you want me to help you to at least try to beat these new allegations."

Snake paces back and forth, then stops. "I gotta better idea. How about we talk about the bullshit you and Odeo pulling behind my back. How much is he paying you Brandon? Tell the truth 'cause I can try to pay you more." Snake says.

Brandon begins putting the documents back inside his briefcase. "Man, I don't know what you're talking about. Guard!"

"Come on, Brandon, man. Don't do this to me. My kids need me. Just name your price! The guard opens the door. Brandon stands, looks at Snake, then walks out.

****

Brandon knocks on the door at Snake's Auto Repair Shop. Odeo opens it and Brandon walks in. After Brandon closes the door, Odeo holds out an envelope. Brandon grabs it but Odeo doesn't release it. "Here's five thousand more. I'll be able to give jou the full twenty G's by the end of da month."

Brandon snatches the envelope. "Come on now man. I told folks I'll have it all by the end of this week…"

"I know, I know, man. But I'm good for it. Man, I got jou, shiiit. Jou 'bout to help me make my career skyrocket," Odeo says, grinning.

"Listen dude…You need to wipe that damn grin off your face because now I gotta front my own shit 'cause *you* comin' up short. You bet not fuck me over," Brandon warns.

Odeo looks hurt. "Come on, man. I'm not. Don't do me like dat. Just work with me on dis. I'm good for my word if no'ting else. No?"

Brandon stares at Odeo a few seconds before walking out.

****

"I stopped by to pay Bruno a visit. This is what he gave me," Brandon says as he opens a purple drawstring bag with the words Crown Royal inscribed on it. He dumps money from it onto the table. There are some hundred-dollar bills but mostly one-dollar bills.

Sli is nodding her head. "Okay. Cool. So, now you got all yo money, right?" Brandon raises his eyebrows. "Guess again." Sli looks at him blinking her eyes.

"It's a total of only fifteen hundred." Sli's mouth drops open. "Yeah…that's what I did." Brandon informs her.

Sli shakes her head. "No that nigga didn't…Okay I'm gonna get in touch with his ass.

Don't worry you'll get all yo money."

Brandon stares at Sli uncomfortably long then wipes his face with his hands. He reaches into his briefcase and pulls out papers. "Who is Big Sheddy, Felanie and Streng, and how are they related to you?"

"Some friends from my neighborhood." "Please tell me that's not their real names."

"I don't know, and I don't give a fuck. But what I really care about is that we need to beat this case. And how are you helping me with that, Brandon?

Brandon takes more notes before dropping his pen onto the desk. "Okay well I'll have to mosey on and make my rounds to the next cells and departments to pay them a visit. By the way, the witnesses who were in that emergency room are saying you were out of control and had them scared to death because they thought you were gonna kill them all."

Sli rolls her eyes in her head. "Come on now. I didn't do anything different than they would've done had one of their kids been sent to a morgue without being properly identified. You can't just tell a mother I think the nameless little Black boy in our morgue is most likely your son." Sli's voice cracks. "We don't know for sure but since we're not showing you his body as proof, we can tell you anything." Tears fall from her eyes, but she quickly wipes themaway.

"Well, maybe had you handled the situation differently some of those incompetent medical workers could be where you are now, and you could be living high off the hog with a huge lawsuit in the making, and this includes the paramedics, who didn't even get the correct spelling of your son's name," Brandon reminds her.

"Oh Pfft! You don't really believe that shit I know." Sli holds out her arms. "Look at my skin color. As long as my ass is Black it'll never be the other way 'round. Even when I'm right, I'm wrong in the white man's world. You know damn well no matter what happens it is and will continue to be a duplex occurrence."

Brandon eyebrows crinkles. "I believe you mean double standards."

Sli widen her eyes, rolls her neck, and turns up her lip. "I said what I said."

Brandon takes more papers from his briefcase. He looks at one. "I have the police report here that says you shot the bullet that killed your mother, Ms. Haddie Maldive. Is this correct?

Sli looks with a blank stare, as flashbacks of her mother's final pleadings for her to put the gun down replays in her mind. Tears fall down her cheeks.

****

A live band is performing at the House of Blues as Brandon and Diana are enjoying dinner and good conversation. After dinner they head to a drive-in theater to watch Enemy of the State. Cars are still pulling in since the movie doesn't start for another thirty minutes. The car radio plays softly as Brandon leans close to Diana to kiss her on the cheek, then the neck. As he is about to kiss her on the lips she tenses. Brandon sits back into his seat and stares out the windshield window. "What's wrong?" He asks.

Diana hesitates before responding. "I'm concerned about my brother. I mean…do you think you'll be able to get him out of there so he can be with his kids, at least by Christmas?"

Brandon turns to face her. "I'm really working on it, baby." He grabs her hand. "Not to sound like a punk or nothing but, and I know you already know this, our judicial system is a lot more complicated than you can ever imagine. It's especially rough on me, being a Black man, trying to help our people because I got in this career specifically for that reason, but it doesn't matter because the powers that be remain just that…regardless of my title for the mere fact that I'm still Black until the day…I was gonna say until I die but even after that I stay on record as being Black, so there's no way around it." They both chuckle. "You may be young, but you know what it's like even being a Black woman in this lifetime. And even though I got fifteen years over you, I can assure you that not much has changed from the time I was born up until your birth date. Well, you didn't have to witness the many marches Martin Luther led for civil rights." Brandon forehead wrinkles. "You know… It's interesting they call it *civil rights*, but it should've been called *Black rights* because we're the only ones who were being deprived of the basic rights that were given naturally to whites, like decent interest rates on car and mortgage loans, safe and clean neighborhoods and don't get me started on the shitty educational system they make us learn in and expect us to still be successful tax paying and back to the law abiding citizens," Brandon says, as he pulls the lever on his seat to lay back placing his forearm across his head. "Okay, granted I was just a little boy, but I still remember watching that Chicago Freedom Movement protest on television." Brandon shakes his head. "It was amazing to see thousands of Blacks walking down one side of the street while whites walked down the other side, for the sake of disrupting our freedom. I mean…all we wanted was the same exact thing whites already had. It never made sense to me that they could be so hell bent on trying to make us continue living in poverty and they did everything they could to make sure it stayed that way." Although Brandon takes a deep breath and blows it out slowly, Diana's shoulders relax as well as she places a hand on Brandon's leg. He looks at her and musters a crooked smile. "I know I went all off topic, but I said all that to say, I'm going to do whatever I can to get your brother out of jail because I know from day one, we're born guilty, about any and everything, just because we're Black." He puts his hand on top of Diana's, squeezing it lovingly. "So now, I'm asking you to please forgive me, baby. This is not the ideal date I had planned forus."

"Naw, it's cool. I'm glad you shared that with me," Diana says, smiling.

The musical interlude of "Fire" by the Pointer Sisters begins playing on the radio. Brandon raises up just enough so he can reach the radio to turn up the volume then lay back down. "I know you don't know nothing about this." He teases Diana.

Diana smacks her lips. "Please…my mom played the Pointer Sisters to death, when she was cooking, in her car, in the shower, and especially when she cleaned the house."

The lyrics begin playing. They both sing along with it, but Diana is acting it out.

I'm ridin' in your car
You turn on the radio
You're pullin' me close
I just say no
I say I don't like it
But you know I'm a liar.
'Cause when we kiss
Ooo…Fire.

Brandon pulls Diana on top of him. They make out, almost through the entire movie.

Later that night they make love at Brandon's house.

CHAPTER 61

Several police cars come to a screeching halt outside of Snake's Auto Shop. Rock lifts his head from under the hood of a car and throws his hands in the air. Officers run out of their cars, rush over to Odeo, grab and handcuff him. "Odeo Santina you're under arrest for a double homicide." He rattles off the Miranda rights. Rock drops his arms and sighs.

Odeo is stunned, fighting to get loose. "Yo! What da fuck. I aint murda no damn body!

Let me go!" As an officer shoves Odeo to the car, he looks over at one of his friends who he hired, and yells, "Yo…hombre, llama a mi esposa¡ Dile que no hice nada¡ Ven a rescatarme¡"

Rock watches, with a huge grin on his face, as they shove Odeo into the back of the police car and drive away.

ONE YEAR LATER

CHAPTER 62

Court has already been in session for weeks. Doctors, nurses, psychiatrist, witnesses, paramedics, attorneys representing the plaintiffs and defendants, the wife of the deceased police officers and police officers themselves have all testified in the combined cases for the police officer who was shot in the head after pulling over the pickup truck, the hostage situation and the shootout at the Cook County hospital, and Bryk's death at Garfield Park, which all occurred on the same night and into the following day. The prosecuting attorney calls up its first surprise witness. "State your full name for the record."

"Theodore Cooper Goins."

"Tell us what you witnessed on the night of July 4 at Garfield Park."

"I saw a young man, Bryk Maldive, get burned to death from exploding fireworks." "And how did that happen?"

"I believe it was the man who was following him, who did it." "Is that man in the courtroom now?"

"Yes."

"Where is he?" The attorney asks then looks in the direction where Ted points.

"Let the record show that Ted Goins points to Odeo Santina as the murderer of Bryk Maldive. The prosecution rests. No further questions your honor."

"Cross examination." The judge says.

The defense attorney, representing Odeo Santina, stands and walks over to Ted. "Mr.

Goins isn't it true that you have different names that you answer to?" "Yes."

"And what are they?"

"Some people call me Ted. Some call me Cooper or Coop." "And why is that?"

"I go by Ted when I'm in professional settings, like work and here at court. Cooper or Coop are my nicknames."

Diana, Snake and Sli look confused.

"So, neither of those names are considered aliases? You're not trying to hide from anyone, or nothing like that?" The attorney facetiously asks.

"Objection!" The prosecuting attorney yells. "Sustained." The judge replies.

"Please tell everyone why you were at Garfield Park on the night of July 4?" "I was selling stuff."

"Please specify. Stuff like what?"

"Socks, towels, bed sheets…mostly necessities and stuff like that." "Oh, so you have a license to sell these things?"

"Objection your honor," yells the prosecuting attorney. "Under what grounds?" Asks the judge.

The prosecuting attorney throws up his hands. "His status has nothing to do with the accusations."

The defense attorney turns to look at the judge. "Integrity has a lot to do with this, your honor." The defense attorney then turns to look at the jury. "If he's selling on the streets, illegally, how can we trust him to be a credible witness in this case?"

The judge nods. "Overruled."

"Again, are you a licensed peddler Mr. Goins?" "No."

"Do you peddle full time or part-time?" "Objection, your honor."

"Sustained." The judge responds.

"What did you do before you became a peddler Mr. Goins?" "Engineer at IBM."

"Why are you no longer working as an engineer at IBM?" "I retired."

"Would you say you're peddling to supplement your retirement pension?" "Well Yeah…um…no."

"Confused much Mr. Goins?" The spectators chuckle. "Which is it?" The judge slams her gavel. "Order in the court."

The prosecuting attorney yells, "Objection your honor! The attorney's badgering the witness."

The defense attorney turns toward the judge. "Your honor I'm getting to my point." "Overruled." The judge responds.

The defense attorney resumes questioning. "Should you even be doing anything as far as work is concerned, Mr. Goins, seeing that you're receiving a disability pension?"

"Objection!" Yells the prosecuting attorney.

"Uh un he don't look disabled to me." Tia says chuckling. Others chuckle with her. "Order in the court." The judge slams her gavel. "Sustained."

"How do you get around when you're peddling or should I say selling, Mr. Goins?" The defense attorney asks.

"I ride a bike."

The defense attorney walks to the table where his seat is, pulls out a photo from a file, then walks back to Ted and shows him.

"Is this you Mr. Goins?" "Yes."

The defense attorney stares at the photograph. "Are you sure this is you, Mr. Goins, because the man in the picture appears to have missing front teeth, an unkempt beard and a sunhat? Are you hiding for some reason because you appear to be wearing a costume here?"

"Objection!" The prosecuting attorney yells. "Sustained." The judge responds.

The defense attorney continues. "I would like to bring into evidence this picture of Mr.

Goins riding a bike with the items he sells piled in a basket and hanging from metal rackets attached to the back of his bike as he peddles, as an illegal peddler through Chicago's west side neighborhoods. Isn't it also true, Mr. Goins, that even though you want everyone to believe that you're poor and possibly homeless you have a five-bedroom home in Oak Park, Illinois and drive this luxurious escalade?" The defense attorney holds up another photo, pans it around the room then gives it to Ted. "I understand there's even a rap you do that's well known among neighborhoods...Let me think...How does it go?"

Tia starts it off. *"Fresh off the freight, so you know it's great! My name is Cooper, but you can call me Coop..."*

"Yes! That's it!" The defense states.

Others in the courtroom join in, in unison, even the judge and bailiff.

Accessories: from bangles, bags to boots.
Got toys for yo' kids that can spin, sang, or shoot.
Wanna eat?
Got those sour, sugary, and salty treats.
Need something at home?
Check out my cutlery, candles, brushes and combs.
If you need it, and I don't got it, just let it be known.
I'll cop it when I can. I SWEAR the wait won't be long.
Be back here in a flash; sangin' this same ole song.

Everyone is laughing and applauding. The judge hammers her gavel, stifling her laughter, is too tickled to say anything. Pictures of Ted on the bike, washing his SUV and standing in front of his home are illuminated on a tv monitor.

People are murmuring. Diana gasps and covers her mouth as tears develop in her eyes.

Snake's and Sli's faces become angry. Ted looks over at Snake, Sli and Diana, then puts his head down.

"Is this home and vehicle yours Mr. Goins?" The defense attorney asks. "Yes." Ted murmurs.

"Could you please speak up Mr. Goins?" "I said yes."

"So, you seem to enjoy making a great living at deceiving people, huh Mr. Goins?" "Objection!" Yells the prosecuting attorney.

"Sustained." The judge says.

The defense attorney moves on. "Wasn't it pretty dark outside on the night that you claim the accused was at Garfield Park?"

"Yes. It was nighttime."

"According to your statement, in the report, you said the accused, and I quote 'Odeo Santina, was wearing a Snap Back cap and sunglasses.' End quote. Is this correct?"

"Yes."

"Then how can you be so sure it was him?"

"He snatched his shades off before he ran over to steal stuff from Bryk's bag, so I got a better look at him. I know it was him because I visited my deceased fiancé's son's auto shop to ask his permission to marry his mother. I recognized Odeo because that's where he works."

The defense attorney stares at Ted then turns his head to address the jury. "Once again I must remind you how could we even believe the testimony of a man who obviously makes a sustainable living deceiving the public and worse, by the looks on the faces of some people in here, even his own loved ones?"

The prosecuting attorney stands up. "Objection!" "Overruled," the judge says.

The defense attorney smirks. "No further questions your honor."

"We'll break for lunch for one hour." The judge says before slamming her gavel.

CHAPTER 63

Court has reconvened. Some people returned fifteen minutes before lunch was over, while others are still trickling in, fifteen minutes late.

The prosecuting attorney begins questioning the second key witness. "State your full name for the record."

"You did say it's okay to use my new government name, right?" The witness squints her eyes. The attorney closes his eyes and nods. "Oh okay…" The witness says then clears her throat. "Tia Navarro." Her voice booms loudly into the microphone. "Where were you on the morning of July 4th?"

"I'm not sure if I was either coming out of or going into the liquor sto' 'cause I had been back and forth over there since I first woke up that day. Tryna get my party on for the holiday. You know what I'm sayin'." She chuckles.

"Please remember to just answer the question, Ms. Navarro. No additional details required."

"Oh yeah that's right okay."

"Did something unusual occur while you were out that day?" "Oh fasho."

"Is that a yes or no, Ms. Navarro?" "Yes."

"Tell us what happened…please."

"I saw some of my neighbors sitting on the sidewalk. I figured the popo was just doing a routine liquor check to see if they had open liquor in the car or maybe they thought the driver had been drinking and driving or something like that. 'Cause you know I've been stopped on some holidays at those certain surprise check points 'cause they wanna see if you wearing yo' seatbelt and sh-stuff like that. But a nig..nice one like me leave 'em lookin' stupid 'cause I know better than to drink and drive 'cause I aint tryna spill my drink. Know what I'm sayin'. Ha ha.

Plus that seatbelt is gon' be tight too. Ha ha. Won't be catchin' my Black a…agnostic self slippin'. 'Cause I always drive away with that cute little sticker they give you after you pass they tests. I guess they wantchu to show er'body you've been a good little boy or girl driver, but I just throw that sh…"

"Ms. Navarro." The prosecuting attorney interrupts.

"Oh yeah answer the question…uh…What was the question?" The audience chuckles. The judge slams her gavel. "Order."

The prosecuting attorney continues. "Please try to stay focused Ms. Navarro. You were saying some of your neighbors…

"Oh yeah so they were all sittin' on the sidewalk when all of a sudden I heard, pop, pop, pop! I had dived to the ground then, once it got quiet, I peeked my head up to see where the shots came from and that's when I saw a black sports car speed off. The license plates said D-A-T M-F Odeo. The reason I remember it is 'cause I kept chanting to myself what the letters stand for— dat muthufucka Odeo, dat muthufucka Odeo, dat…" The audience chuckles.

The judge slams her gavel. "Ms. Navarro if you don't watch your language, you will be banned from this courtroom." The defense attorney chuckles as he writes on a pad.

"Ms. Navarro, please!" The prosecuting attorney says as he drops his arms. "Okay daaang." Tia says as she shifts in her seat.

The judge raises her eyebrows as she looks at Tia. Tia looks back her with raised eyebrows then rolls her eyes before continuing to speak. "Anyway, I see this same vehicle in the neighborhood all the time. So when I stood up, I saw a cop laying on the ground and all the cops going crazy talkin' about they been set up 'cause an officer had got shot in the head. When I heard one of them say 'secure the area.'" Tia's changes her voice mocking a white man's, then goes back to her normal voice as she continues. "I hurried up and got outta there 'cause I didn't want them holding me up for long hours for something I didn't do. Then later that day it hit me. I remembered I saw my neighbors was out in the yard building something, the night before, when that same car had pulled up in the alley behind my neighbor's house. The driver sounded Hispanic when he yelled out the window." Tia changes her voice, mocking a Hispanic accent. "'Tell Snake tank jou, he owe me one, he welcome.' Or something like that."

Sli, Big Sheddy, Streng and Felanie exchange glances as they sit listening, handcuffed and in their prison uniforms. Snake avoids looking at any of them as he shakes his head.

The prosecuting attorney walks over to a table to retrieve a photo then walks back to show it to Tia. "Is this the same car and license plates you saw?"

"Heeell yeah it is! That's the one! Oops, I mean yes."

"Let the photo be entered as evidence that the vehicle in question is registered to Odeo Santina."

The Judge turns to the defense attorney, "You cross examining this one?"

The defense attorney has his elbows leaning on the table as he doodles on a pad with one hand while his free hand is cropped under his chin, doesn't bother to even look up. "No thank you, your honor. The defense rests."

"This will conclude our court session for today. Hopefully the jury will have determined the verdict before the morning. Please return back here tomorrow at 9:00 a.m. Court is adjourned." The judge slams her gavel.

The sound of rustling bodies reverberates throughout the courtroom as people are standing and moving about, preparing to leave.

CHAPTER 64

Promptly at 9:00 a.m., the next morning, the bailiff announces. "Court is now in session.

All rise for the honorable Judge Lana Chetkowski!" Everyone, who is able, stands. When the judge takes her seat the bailiff yells, "You may be seated!"

"I understand the jury has reached a verdict?"

"Yes, your honor." A representative of the jury replies. "What have you determined?"

"We the jury have determined that Streng Bean Turner, Earl "Big Sheddy" Mac and Felanie Gunay Burns are each found to be guilty on one count of accessory of attempted murder of Tawny Maldive."

Loud gasps and protests are heard in the court. The judge hits her gavel on her desk. "Order in the court!"

"We the jury find Odeo Santina is not guilty of the murder of a police officer." Sighs of relief is heard from several people, while some are yelling out in anger.

"We the jury find Odeo Santina guilty on one count of the unintentional murder ofa minor, Bryk Maldive." People are yelling in disagreement and sobbing in shock. The judge repetitively slams the gavel."Silence!"

"We the jury find Shilange Sli Maldive guilty of one count of attempted murder of Tawny Maldive. Also, guilty on one count of the unintentional murder of Haddie Maldive." Loud gasps and protests are heard in the court.

Sli who was looking down at the floor looks up at the jury stunned. "Nooooo!" She screams.

"Ahahaha…That's what you get!" Snake yells.

The judge whacks her gavel, several times, on the bench. "Settle down everyone!"

"We the jury find Renault Snake Maldive guilty on one count for first-degree murder of Grenely Brown." People are yelling in disagreement and sobbing in shock.

"What! I didn't kill no Grenely! Sli, you know damn well you did that!" Snake yells. Sli smiles deviously as she stares at Snake.

The judge repetitively slams the gavel. "Order!"

Loud gasps and protests continue. The judge stands up and drops her gavel on the bench. "Shut the fuck up!" Everyone goes silent as they stare at her; some with disdain and others with fear, as several look away covering their mouths to muffle chuckles.

The judge plops back down in her seat before continuing. "We shall begin the sentencings. I am ordering total silence until the final reading is complete. If anybody so much as sneezes before I'm finished reading, bailiff, you have my permission to escort them out. How you do it is none of my concern. I hereby sentence Streng Bean Turner, Earl "Big Sheddy" Mac and Felanie Gunay Burns each to spend three years on house arrest due to one count of accessory of attempted murder of TawnyMaldive."

"I hereby sentence Odeo Santina to three years house arrest due to one count of the unintentional murder of a minor. Nope. Scratch that. He looks like the type that would murder a police officer if given the chance so let's make that four years house arrest." She looks around the room over the top of her glasses. "I know it wasn't proven but that's not to say he didn't do it."

"I hereby sentence Shilange Sli Maldive to a total of ten years in the Piotrków Poland Prison." The judge pronounces it in with a Poland accent. "Where you are wanted for previous criminal activities. You will be returned to the United States, as the Polish officials see fit, to serve the remainder of whatever time is left for the attempted murder of your niece, Tawny Maldive and second-degree murder of Haddie Maldive."

People are yelling in disagreement and sobbing in shock. Even Nicky loudly smacks her lips and looks at the judge with a frown. The judge repetitively slams the gavel, then looking over the top of her glasses she turns her attention toward Nicky, giving her that Sista girl look. The bailiff pulls a person from their seat, as they continue protesting, he pushes them out the door.

Sli yells out, "What! Nooooo!" She falls to her knees. "You got one mo' again!" The judge yells.

Sli ignores her. "Noooooo! Oh God no! This is not how this was supposed to go! Nicky, you bitch, you promised me!" Sli sobs loudly.

"I said what I said!" The judge rolls her eyes as she continues. "I hereby sentence Renault Snake Maldive to twenty years in maximum security at the Danli Prison in Honduras for first- degree murder of Grenely Brown. I hope you know something about farming. I can't believe they still don't have running water. Oh, but you already know that because you've visited there before, where you've committed other crimes." The judge gives Snake a snide look. "Court is adjourned!"

"What! I've never been there a day in my life! You crooked ass judge!" Snake, Sli, Odeo and Nicky all look at Brandon festering with anger.

CHAPTER 65

Brandon, Rock, Diana, Tawny, Tyler and Nicky are standing along the wall outside the courtroom as security officers escort Sli out. Sli is in tears. Nicky is tearing up as she stares at Sli. Marcus and another security officer are escorting Snake past those aligned along the wall.

Snake glares at Brandon. "Man, I can't believe you did this shit to me!"

Rock throws up a fist to get Snake's attention. "No worries dog. I got you." Rock pounds his chest. "I'll hold down the shop 'til you get out," Rock assures Snake.

Snake looks at Rock with gratitude, then at his family with compassion. "Take care of my family man," he pleads to Rock.

Rock nods. "Fasho, man."

Snake looks at Brandon with contempt. "I'll be back out before you can get too comfortable dude."

"Hey Nicolas!" Marcus yells out.

Nicky looks stunned, widening her eyes, in hopes of getting Marcus to shut up. "Who you talkin' to, Marcus!" Nicky's face crinkles.

"You gone be Nicolas to me until those hormones make your boobs a size double D and you finally get that thang chopped completely off."

Brandon looks at Nicky with confusion then at Marcus. Nicky gets in Marcus's face whispering loudly between clenched teeth. "Shut the fuck up, Marcus!"

Marcus smacks his lips and gets louder. "Maaan…how you gone be embarrassed about who you claim to be. So, now you just confirmed you still taping your joint down, huh. Whatchu waiting on to gone get it chopped off anyway?

Brandon looks pissed, then sick before bending over to vomit.

Marcus frowns. "Ooooh…Daaamn dooog…Looks like somebody done messed around and let Nicolas wax his shit? See now if you had done a reach around you would've learned before now that he still didn't get that surgery yet!" Marcus laughs diabolically.

CHAPTER 66

"Them mufukas'll be here soon. I need yall to remind them why they no longer welcomed here." Rock says, sitting at Snake's desk, addressing five men who are sitting and standing around him.

One of them cocks a sawed off shot gun. Rock smiles. "Yeah, that'll do it."

A car pulls up with three guys sitting inside. The engine shuts off. The car doors open as the three guys are about to step out the car. Rock and the five men stand up and walk outside.

The five guys point guns at the men standing outside the car. Rock steps forward.

"Oh, I guess you mufukas ain't get the memo… ¡Estás despedido, estúpido cabrón!" The three guys stand there staring, stunned.

"Oh, you mufukas still confused? Okay allow me to translate this shit differently: Quedate el culo in Humboldt Park hijo de puta! And I bet not see yall ugly asses around here no mo'!" The man with the sawed off shot gun shoots twice toward the sky.

The three guys hurry to get back inside the car and drive off. Rock runs to his office. A few seconds later he's back outside with square plats in his hand. "Hey yo one of yall grab that ladder and lean it against that pole."

Rock climbs the ladder and covers Snake's name with his so that it reads "Rock's Auto Repair." After climbing back down, he dusts his hands against each.

"A'ight…Now we are officially back in business, under new management. You know the drill ladies—two on, three off."

Two of the men stand outside taking a security officer's stance, glancing around the area, while the other three go under the hoods of cars, repairing them.

Rock walks back inside, turns the *OPEN* sign on and sits down, pecking away at the computer.

Everyone needs a little help sometimes.

Suicide:
CALL: 1-800-273-8255
OR
TEXT: HELLO TO 741741

Domestic Violence:
CALL: 1-800-799-7233
OR
TEXT: SUPPORT TO 741741

Bullying:
1-800-420-1479
OR
TEXT: HOME TO 741741

Self Harm:
CALL: 1-800-366-8288
OR
TEXT: CONNECT TO 741741

LGBTQ+:
CALL: 1-866-488-7386
OR
TEXT: START TO 678678

Sexual Assault:
CALL: 1-800-656-4673
OR
TEXT: HOME TO 741741

Abortion:
CALL: 1-866-439-4253
OR
TEXT: HELPLINE TO 313131

Pregnancy Infant & Child Loss:
CALL: 1-800-944-4773
OR
TEXT: HELLO TO 741741

Grief:
CALL: 1-800-445-4808
OR
TEXT: CARE TO 839863

Eating Disorders:
CALL: 1-800-931-2237
OR
TEXT: NEDA TO 741741

For more hotlines & resources visit:
GRIEFRESOURCENETWORK.COM

Mental Health:
CALL: 1-800-950-6264
OR
TEXT: NAMI TO 741741